BRETT BEAN

ZOO PATROL SQUAD

KINGDOM CAPER

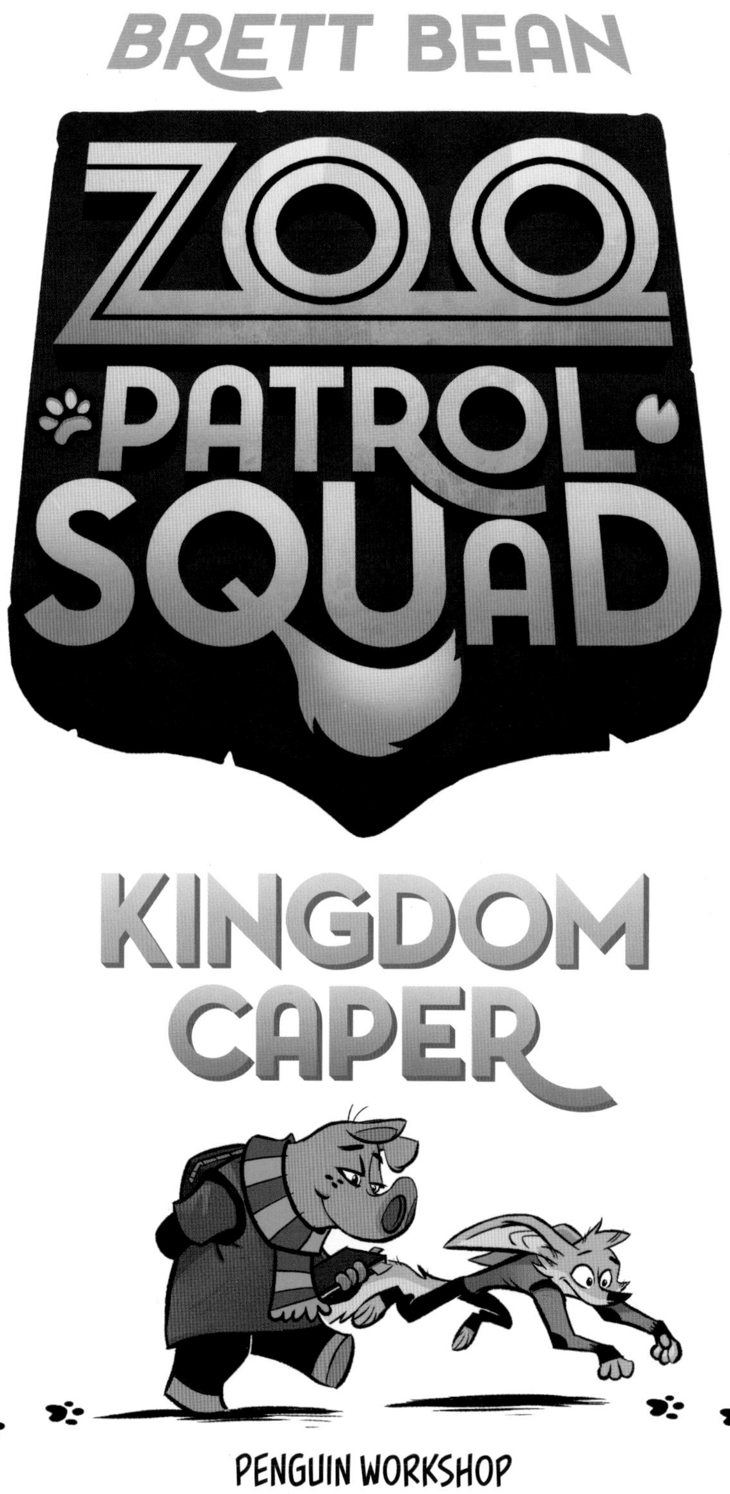

PENGUIN WORKSHOP

NOTE FROM THE AUTHOR

Special thanks to my wife, Julie, for the support it takes to create this world; my boys, Finnegan and Tobbin, for being a source of constant energy; and to Rob Valois and Alex Wolfe who helped bring this story out of me.

To my family and yours. Dream, wonder, and wander.

ABOUT THE CREATOR

Brett Bean is an author, illustrator, and designer whose work has been featured across film, TV, comics, children's books, and more. He has lots of artwork and designs on his website, brettbean.com.
He works from Los Angeles.

To learn more about the Zoo Patrol Squad, go to zoopatrolsquad.com.

W

PENGUIN WORKSHOP
An Imprint of Penguin Random House LLC, New York

Penguin supports copyright. Copyright fuels creativity, encourages diverse voices, promotes free speech, and creates a vibrant culture. Thank you for buying an authorized edition of this book and for complying with copyright laws by not reproducing, scanning, or distributing any part of it in any form without permission. You are supporting writers and allowing Penguin to continue to publish books for every reader.

The publisher does not have any control over and does not assume any responsibility for author or third-party websites or their content.

Copyright © 2020 by Brett Bean. All rights reserved. Published by Penguin Workshop, an imprint of Penguin Random House LLC, New York. PENGUIN and PENGUIN WORKSHOP are trademarks of Penguin Books Ltd, and the W colophon is a registered trademark of Penguin Random House LLC. Manufactured in China.

Visit us online at www.penguinrandomhouse.com.

Library of Congress Control Number: 2020002239

ISBN 9780593093702   10 9 8 7 6 5 4 3 2 1

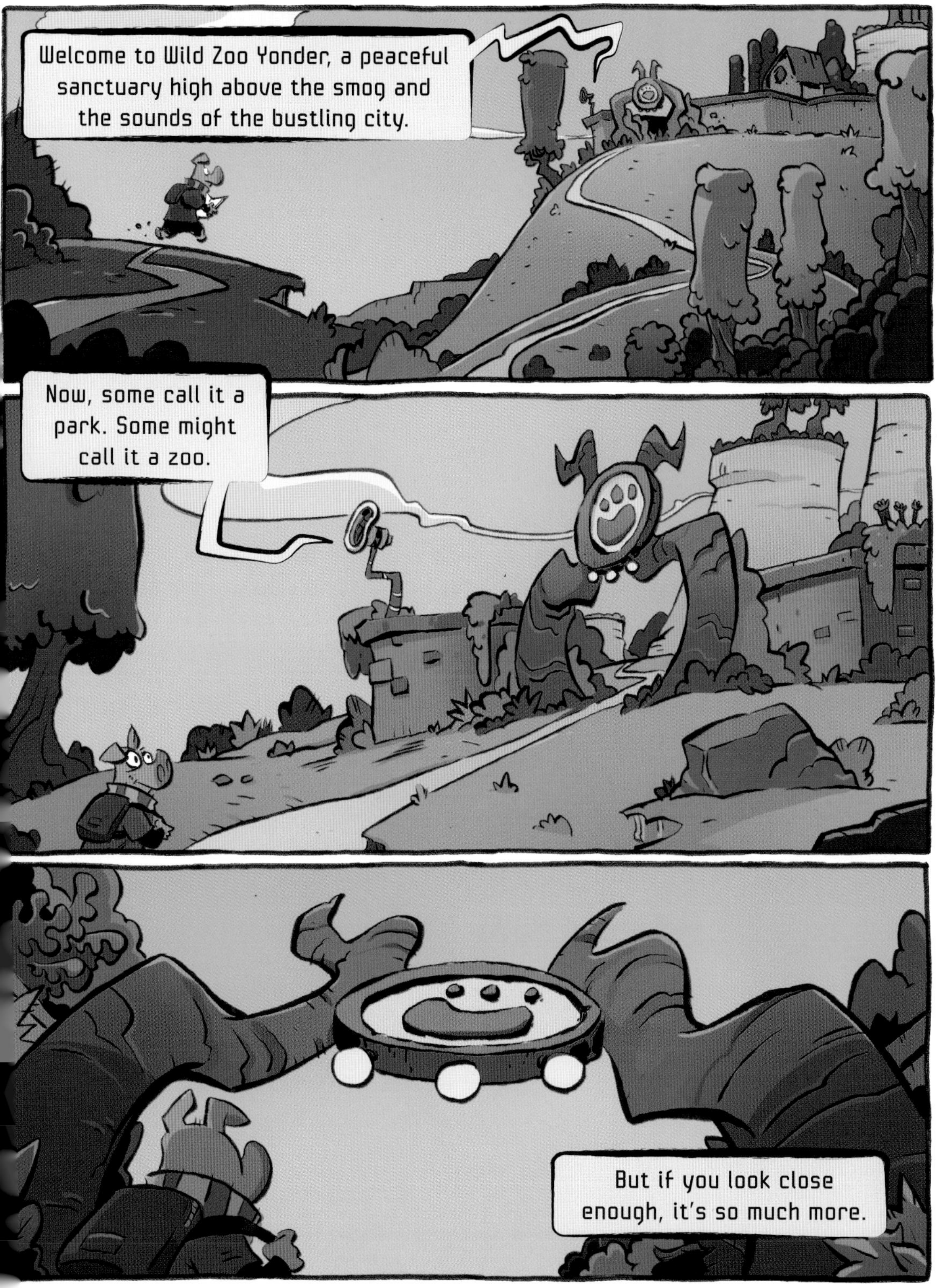
Welcome to Wild Zoo Yonder, a peaceful sanctuary high above the smog and the sounds of the bustling city.
Now, some call it a park. Some might call it a zoo.
But if you look close enough, it's so much more.

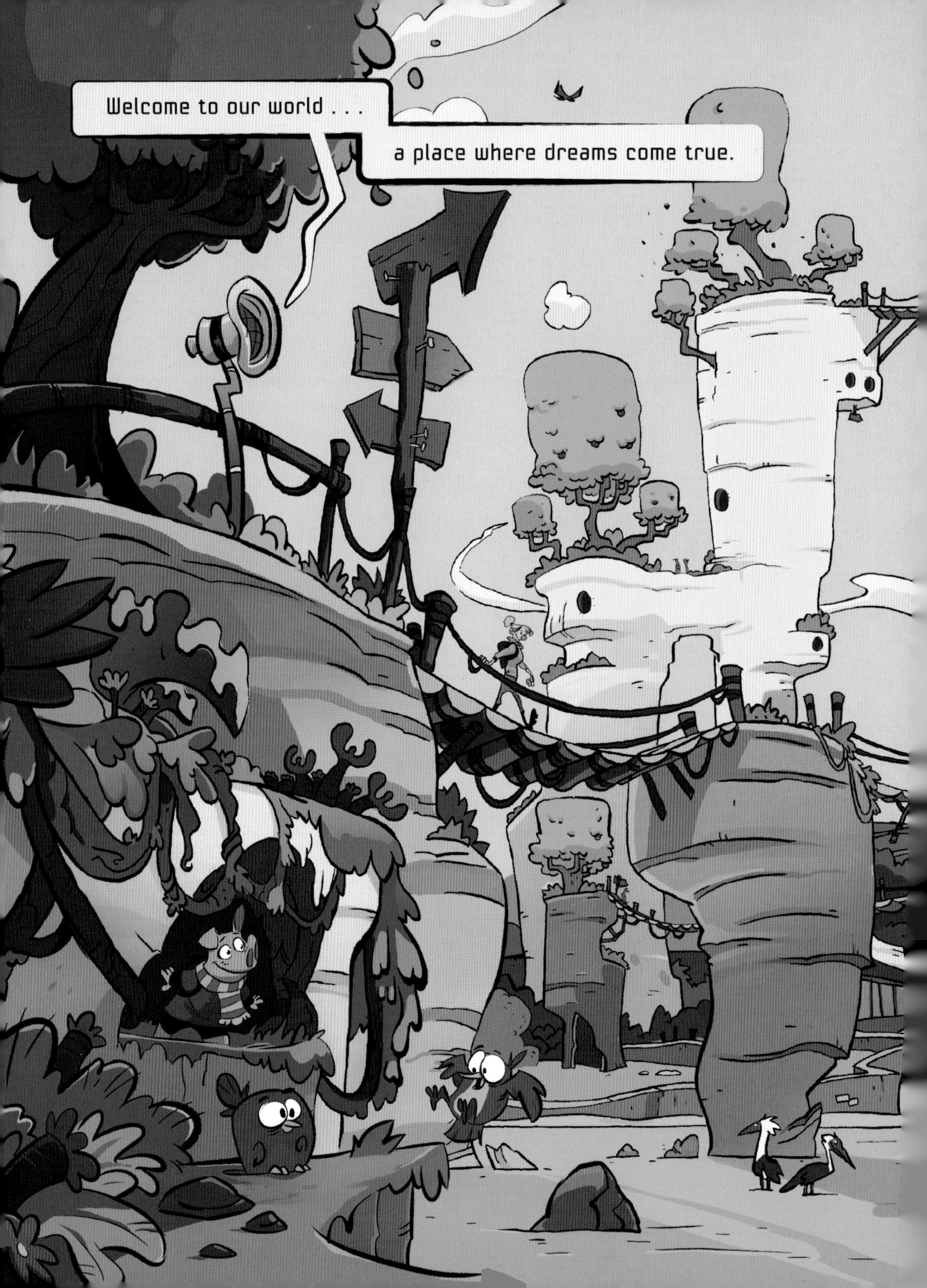
Welcome to our world . . .
a place where dreams come true.

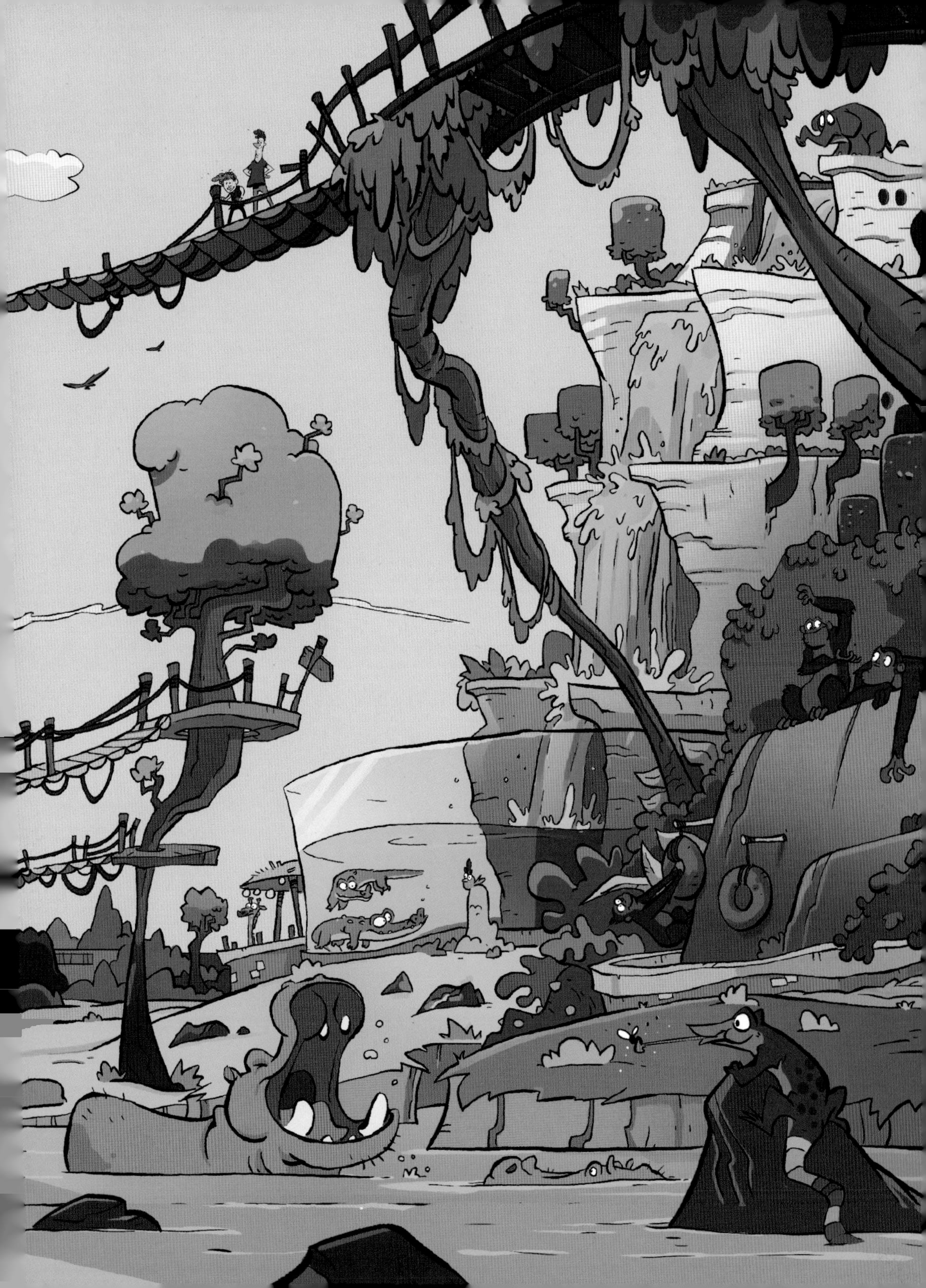

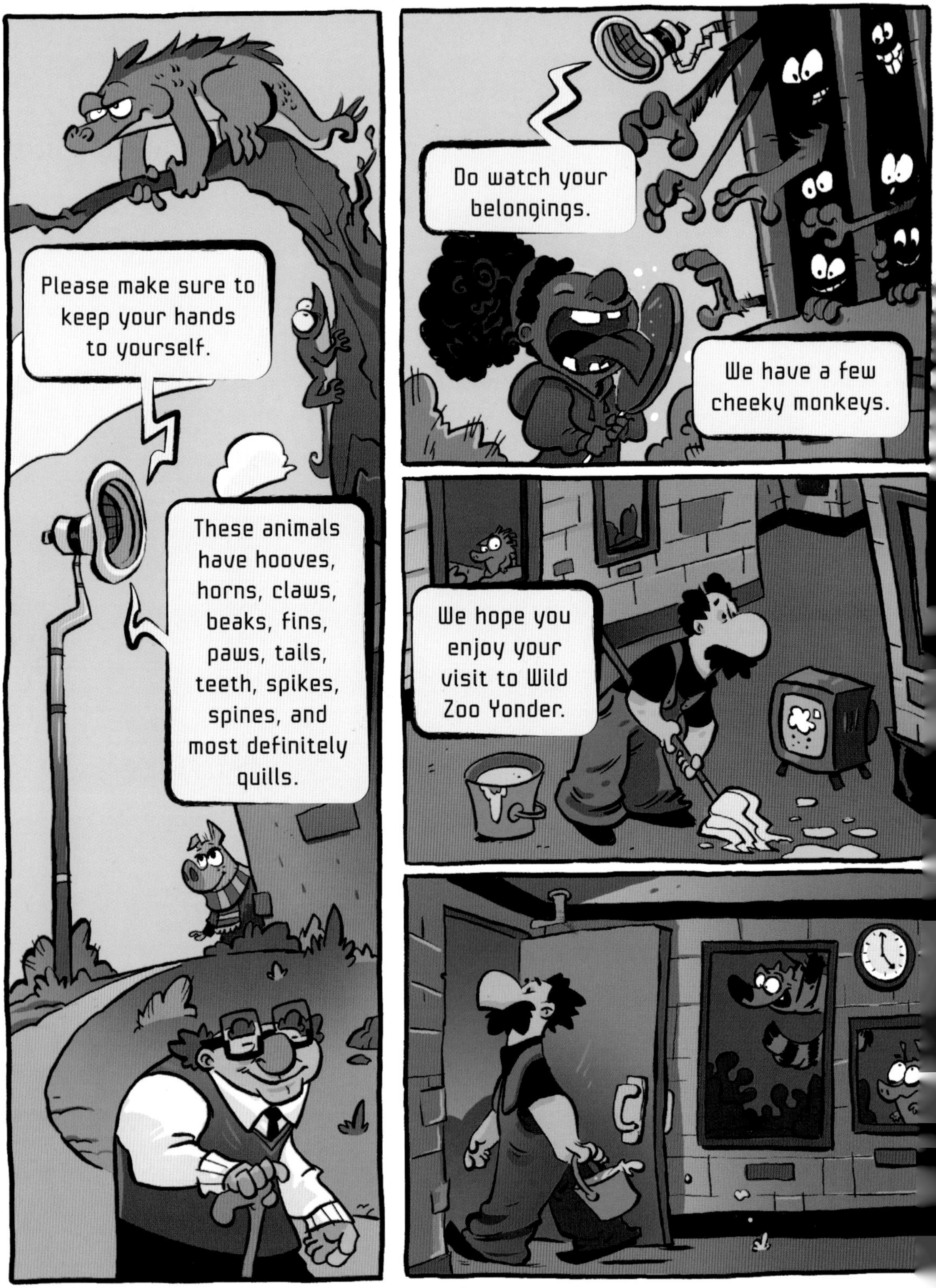
Please make sure to keep your hands to yourself.
These animals have hooves, horns, claws, beaks, fins, paws, tails, teeth, spikes, spines, and most definitely quills.
Do watch your belongings.
We have a few cheeky monkeys.
We hope you enjoy your visit to Wild Zoo Yonder.

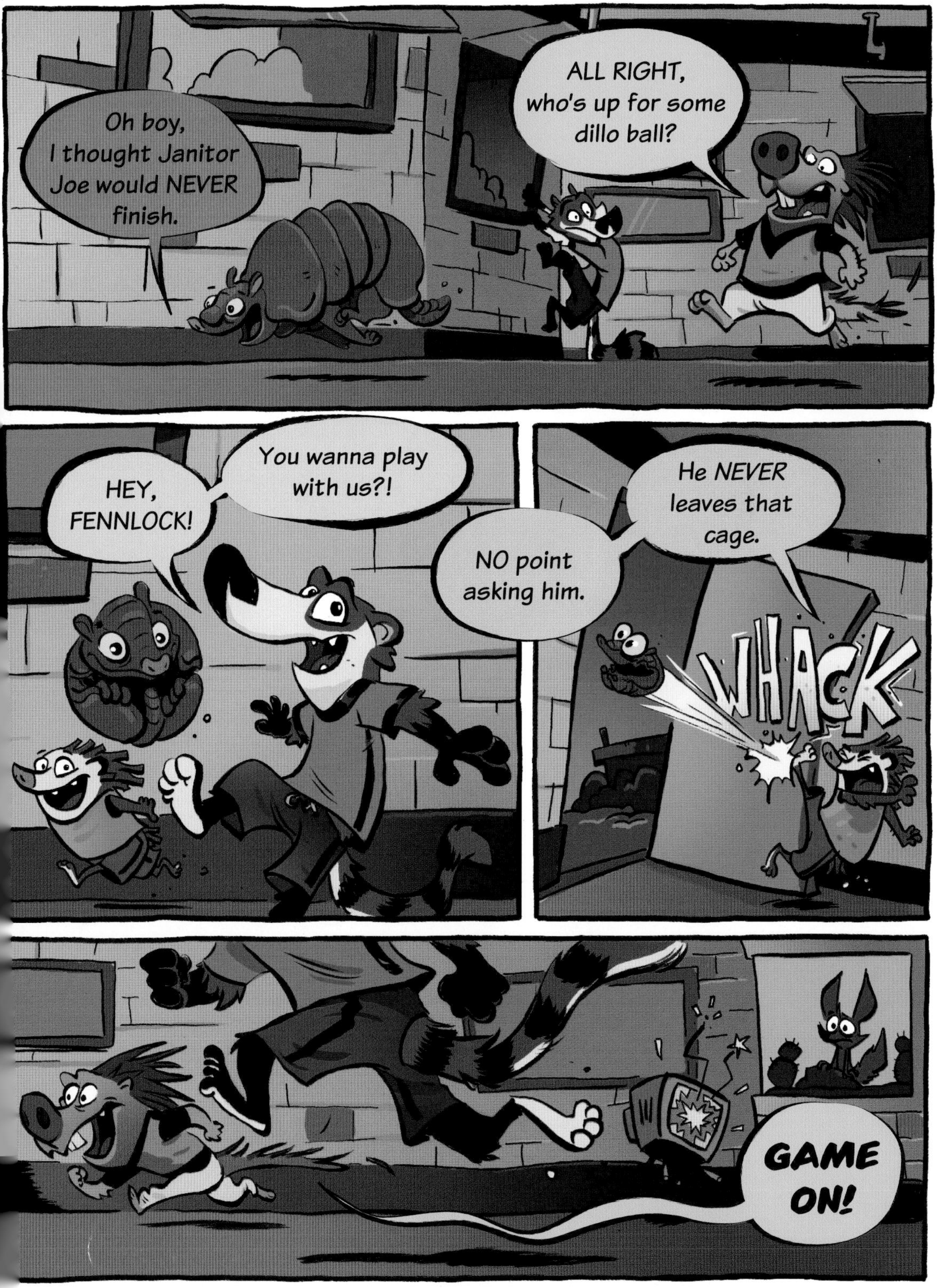
Oh boy, I thought Janitor Joe would NEVER finish.
ALL RIGHT, who's up for some dillo ball?
HEY, FENNLOCK!
You wanna play with us?!
NO point asking him.
He NEVER leaves that cage.
WHACK
GAME ON!

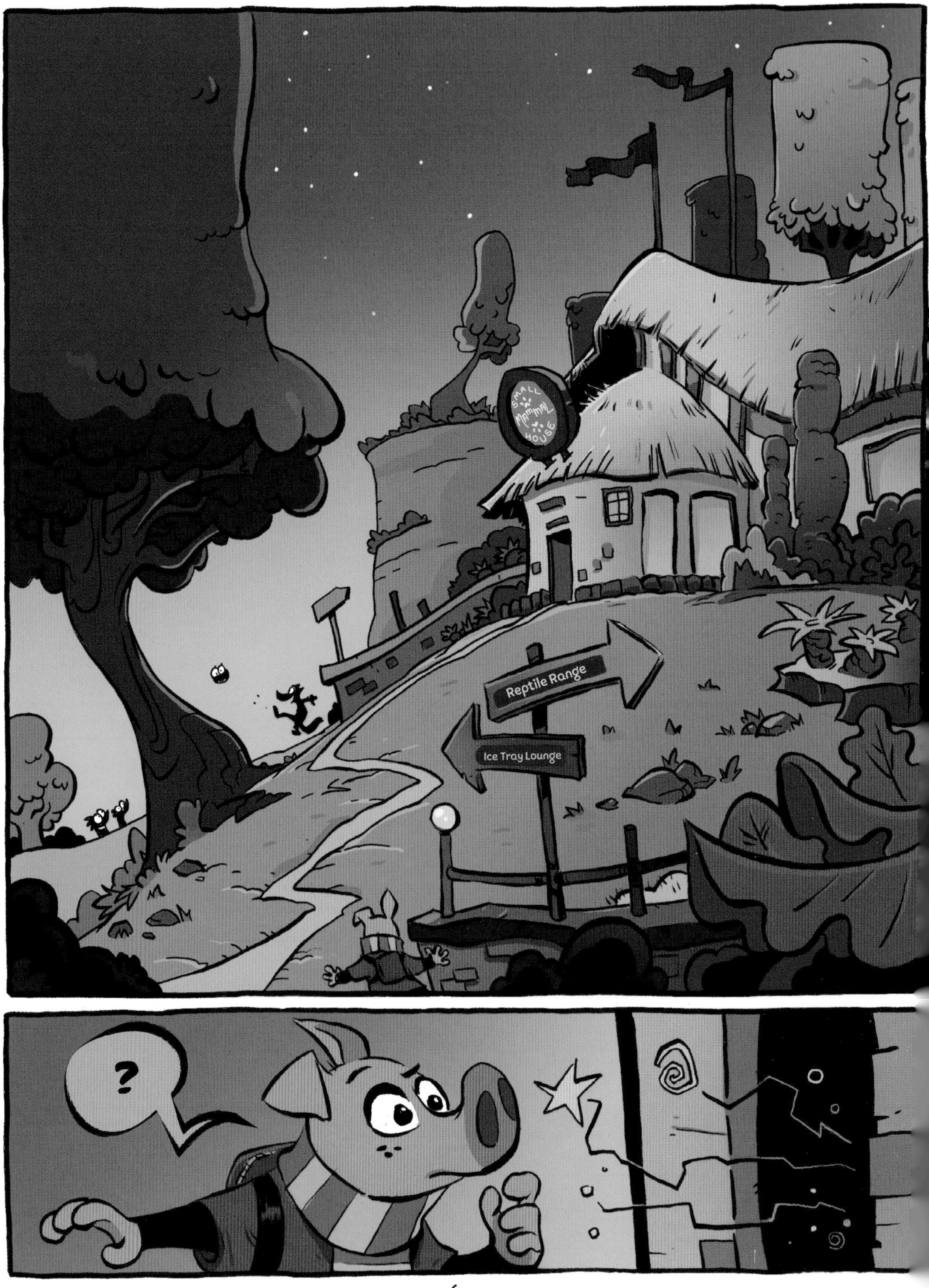
SMALL MAMMAL HOUSE
Reptile Range
Ice Tray Lounge
?

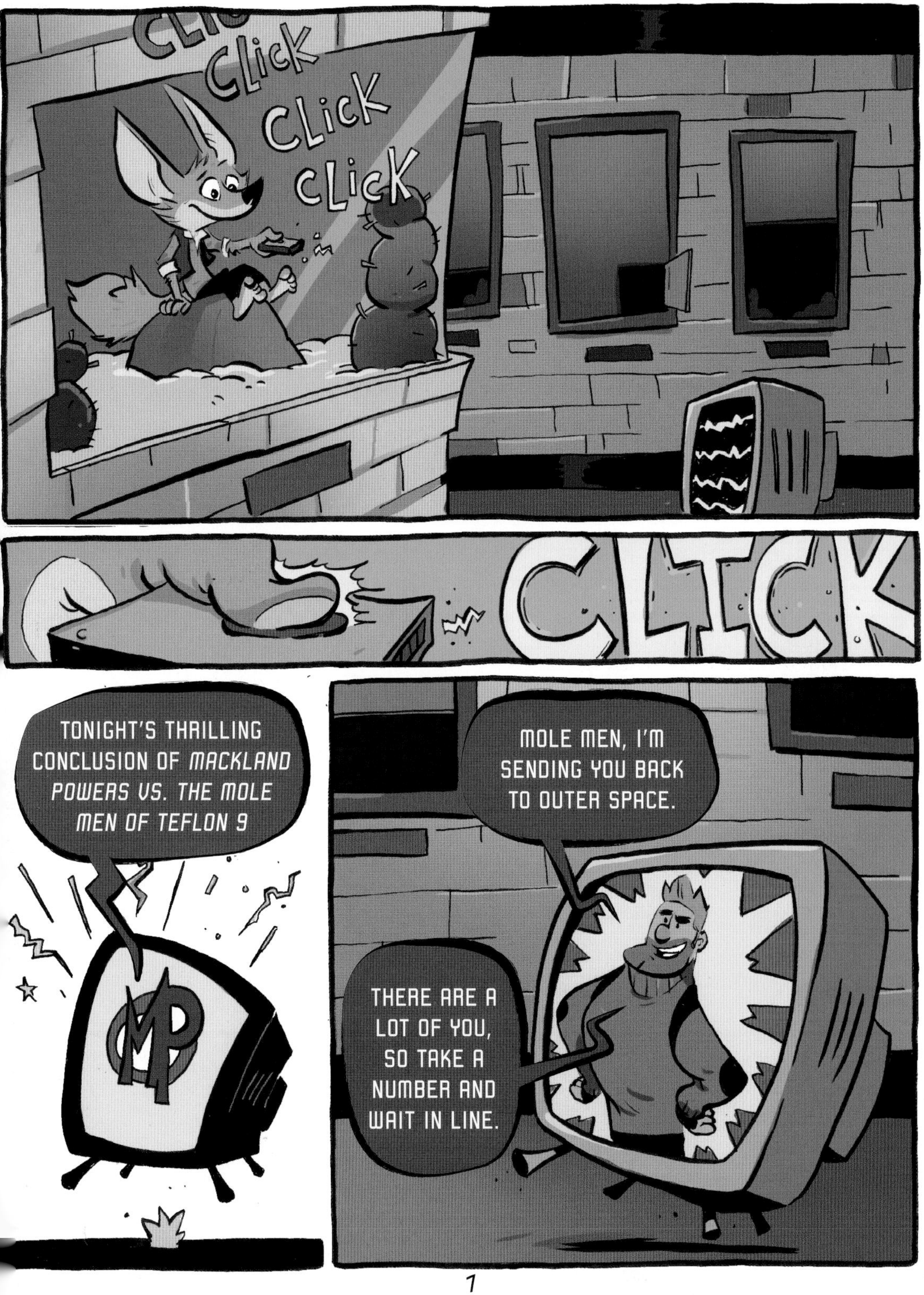
CLICK
CLICK
CLICK
CLICK
TONIGHT'S THRILLING CONCLUSION OF *MACKLAND POWERS VS. THE MOLE MEN OF TEFLON 9*
MOLE MEN, I'M SENDING YOU BACK TO OUTER SPACE.
THERE ARE A LOT OF YOU, SO TAKE A NUMBER AND WAIT IN LINE.

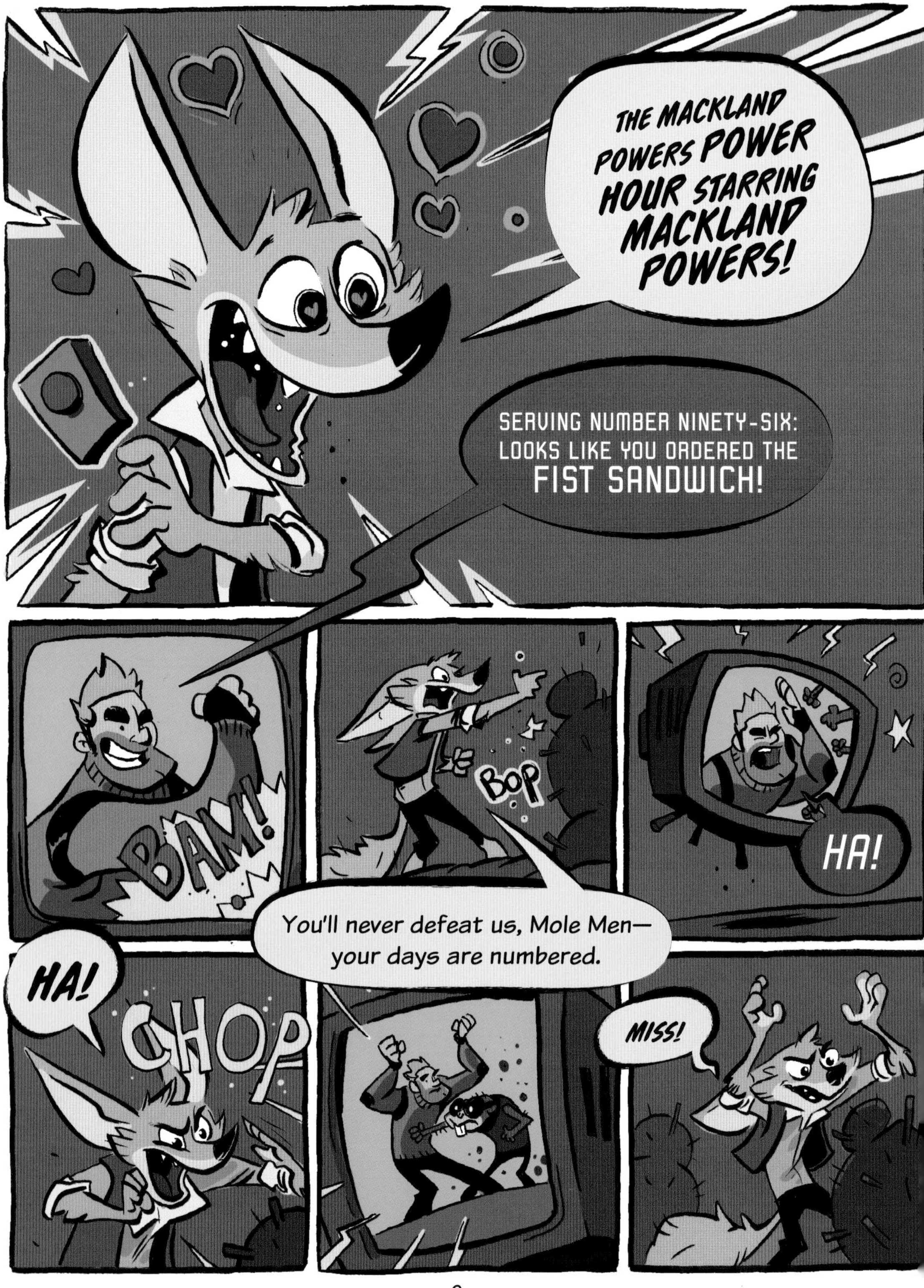
THE MACKLAND POWERS POWER HOUR STARRING MACKLAND POWERS!
SERVING NUMBER NINETY-SIX: LOOKS LIKE YOU ORDERED THE FIST SANDWICH!
BAM!
BOP
HA!
You'll never defeat us, Mole Men—your days are numbered.
HA!
CHOP
MISS!

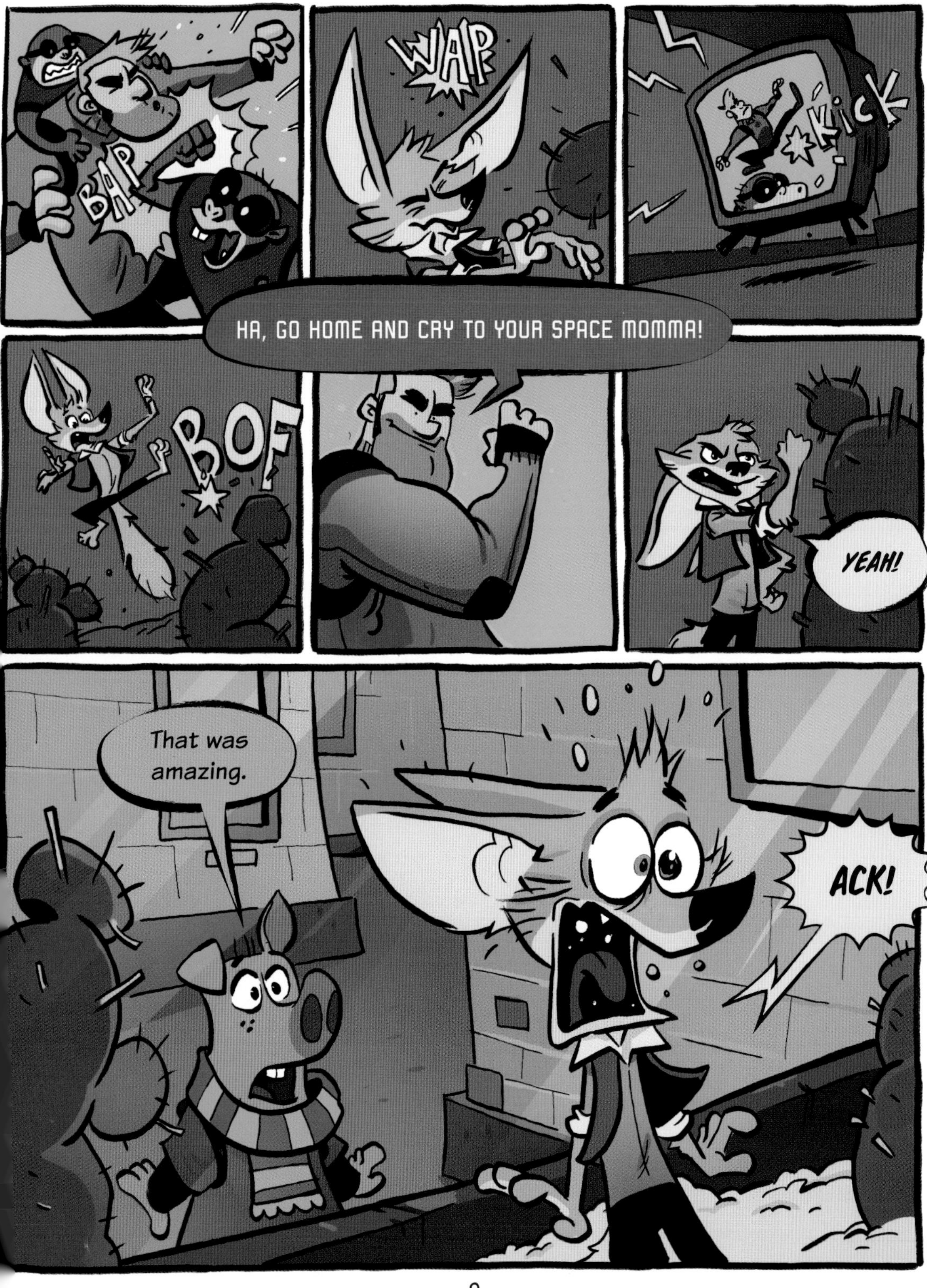
BAP
WAP
KICK
HA, GO HOME AND CRY TO YOUR SPACE MOMMA!
BOF
YEAH!
That was amazing.
ACK!

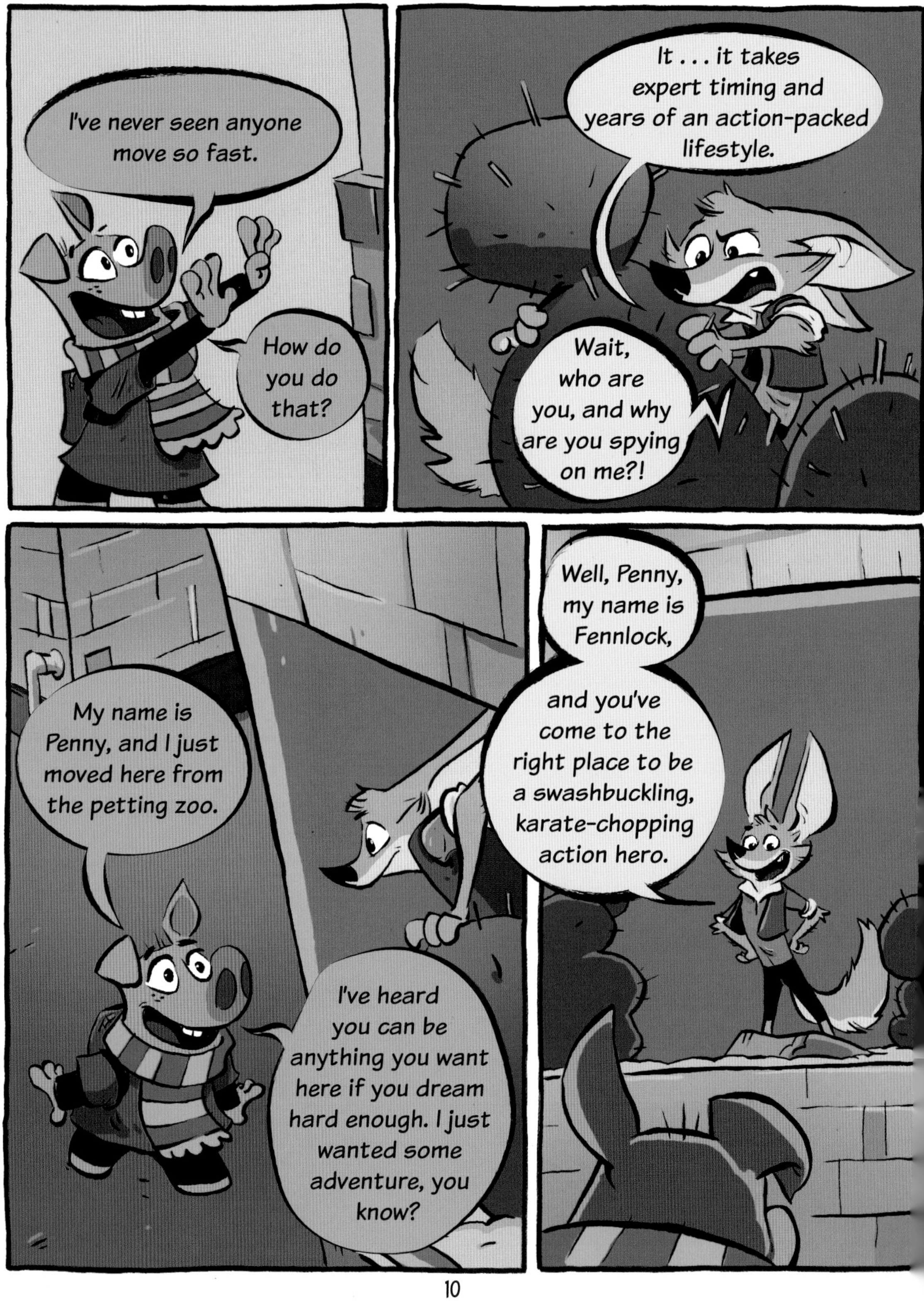
I've never seen anyone move so fast.
How do you do that?
It . . . it takes expert timing and years of an action-packed lifestyle.
Wait, who are you, and why are you spying on me?!
My name is Penny, and I just moved here from the petting zoo.
I've heard you can be anything you want here if you dream hard enough. I just wanted some adventure, you know?
Well, Penny, my name is Fennlock,
and you've come to the right place to be a swashbuckling, karate-chopping action hero.

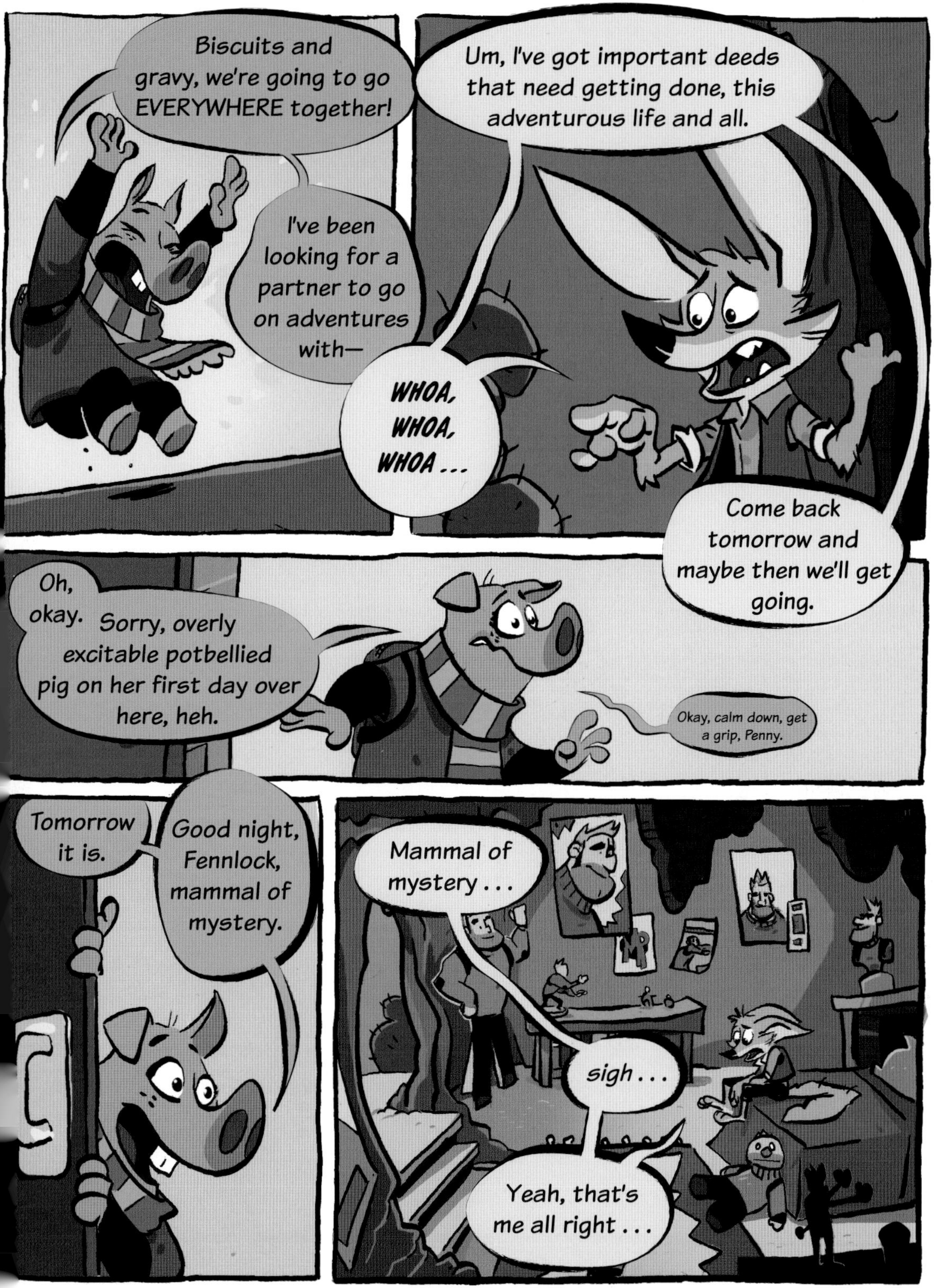
Biscuits and gravy, we're going to go EVERYWHERE together!
I've been looking for a partner to go on adventures with—
Um, I've got important deeds that need getting done, this adventurous life and all.
WHOA, WHOA, WHOA . . .
Come back tomorrow and maybe then we'll get going.
Oh, okay.
Sorry, overly excitable potbellied pig on her first day over here, heh.
Okay, calm down, get a grip, Penny.
Tomorrow it is.
Good night, Fennlock, mammal of mystery.
Mammal of mystery . . .
sigh . . .
Yeah, that's me all right . . .

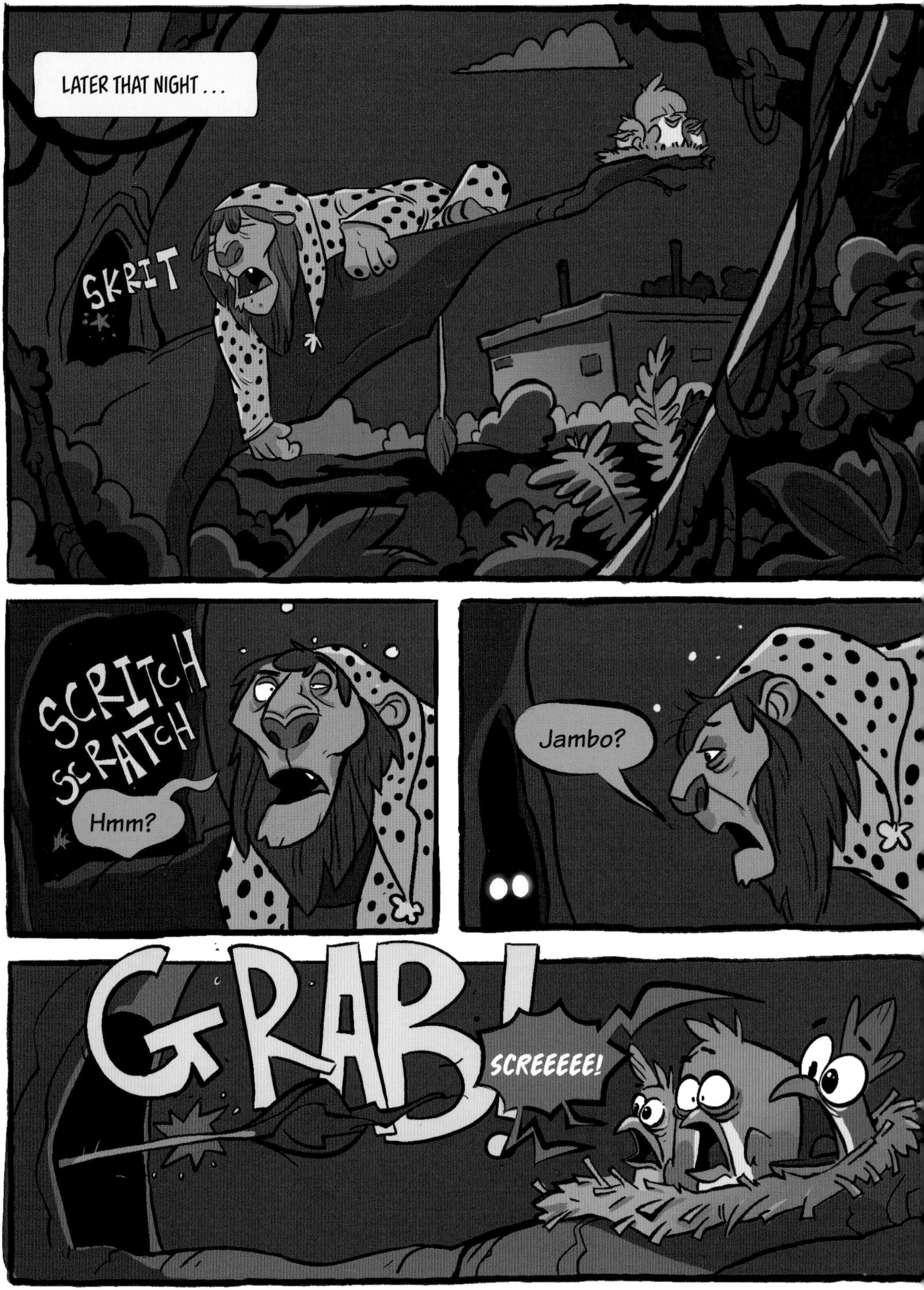
LATER THAT NIGHT . . .
SKRIT
SCRITCH SCRATCH
Hmm?
Jambo?
GRAB!
SCREEEEE!

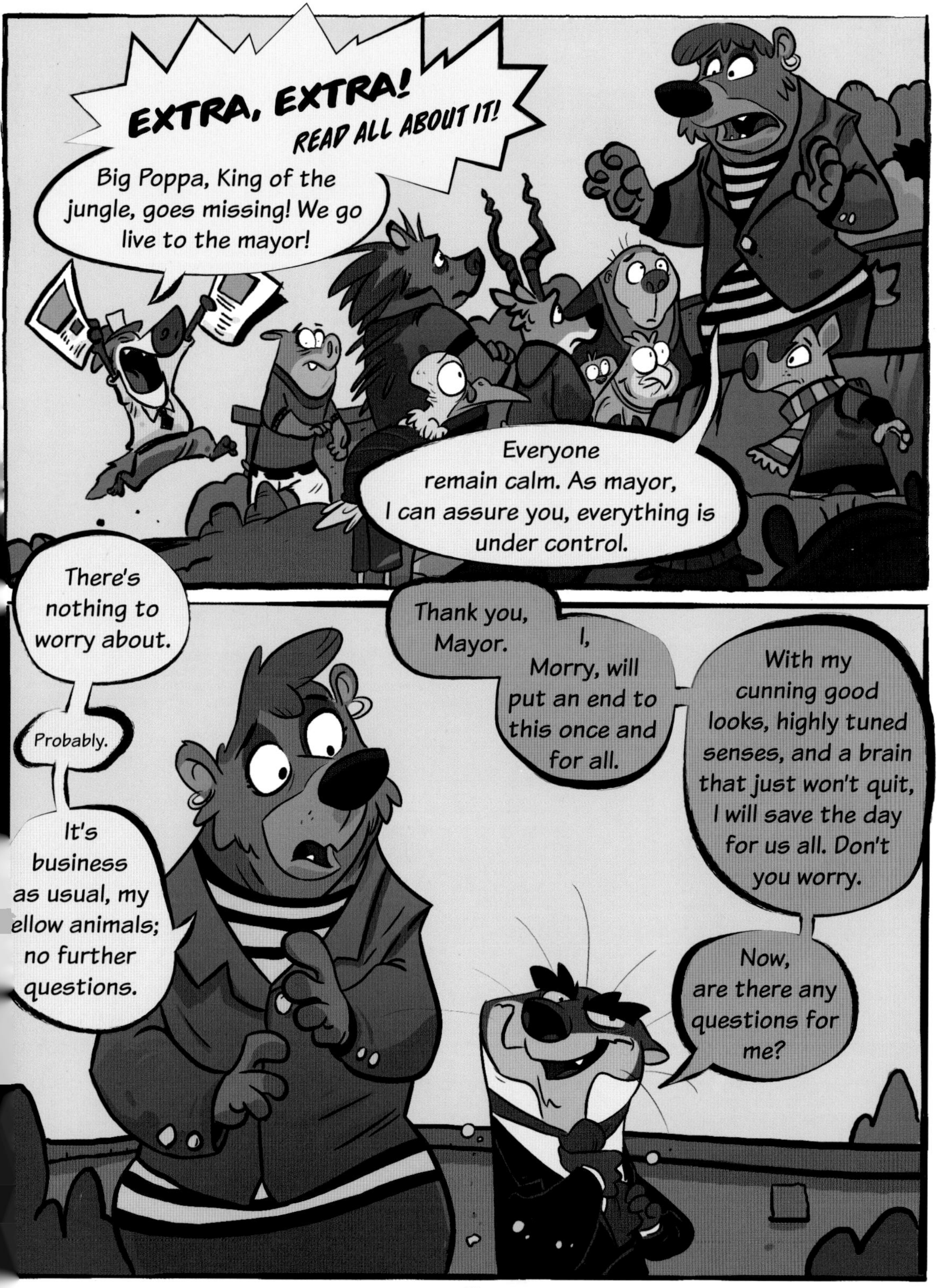
EXTRA, EXTRA! READ ALL ABOUT IT!
Big Poppa, King of the jungle, goes missing! We go live to the mayor!
Everyone remain calm. As mayor, I can assure you, everything is under control.
There's nothing to worry about.
Probably.
It's business as usual, my ellow animals; no further questions.
Thank you, Mayor.
I, Morry, will put an end to this once and for all.
With my cunning good looks, highly tuned senses, and a brain that just won't quit, I will save the day for us all. Don't you worry.
Now, are there any questions for me?

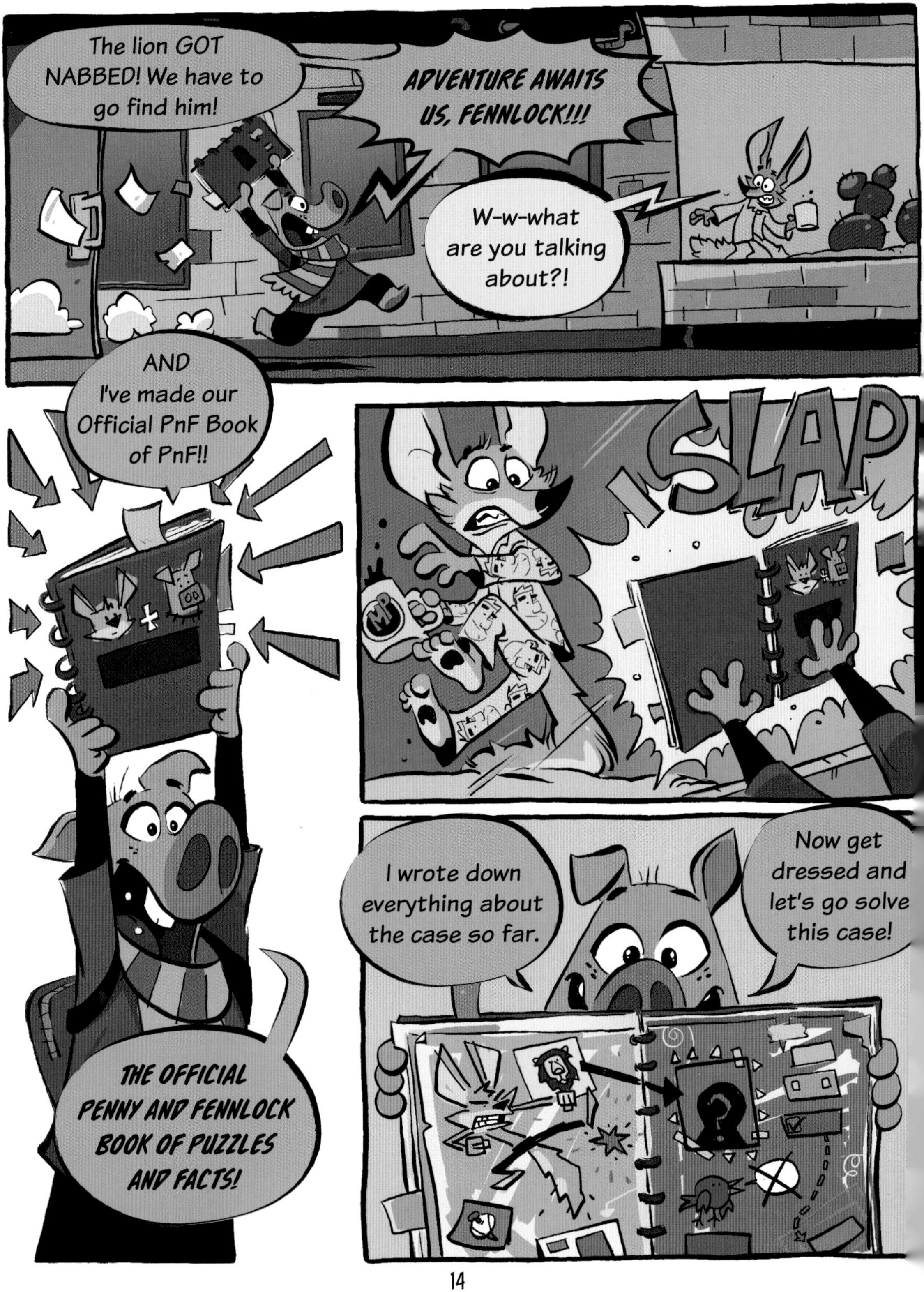
The lion GOT NABBED! We have to go find him!
ADVENTURE AWAITS US, FENNLOCK!!!
W-w-what are you talking about?!
AND I've made our Official PnF Book of PnF!!
THE OFFICIAL PENNY AND FENNLOCK BOOK OF PUZZLES AND FACTS!
SLAP
MP
I wrote down everything about the case so far.
Now get dressed and let's go solve this case!

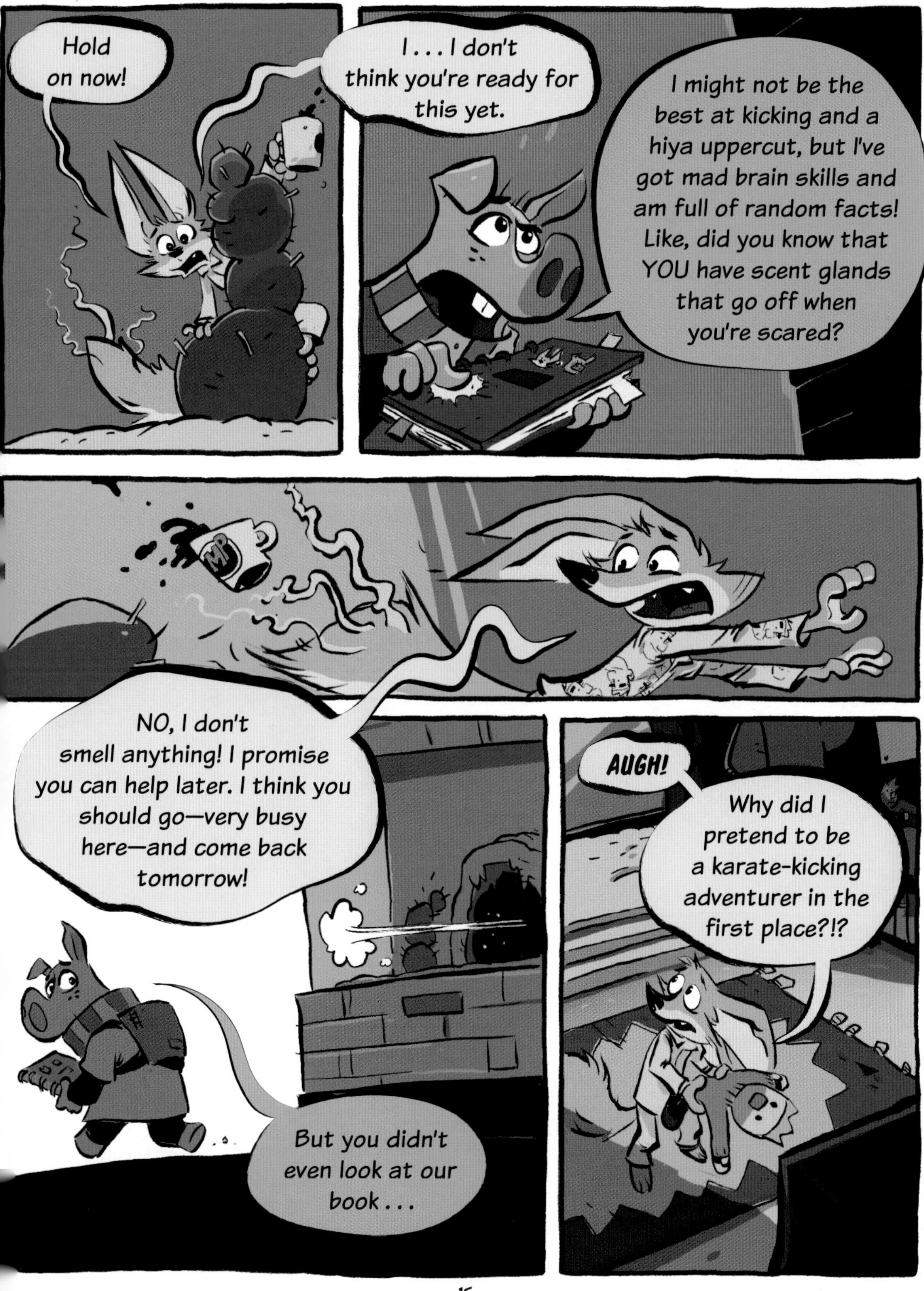
Hold on now!
I . . . I don't think you're ready for this yet.
I might not be the best at kicking and a hiya uppercut, but I've got mad brain skills and am full of random facts! Like, did you know that YOU have scent glands that go off when you're scared?
NO, I don't smell anything! I promise you can help later. I think you should go—very busy here—and come back tomorrow!
But you didn't even look at our book . . .
AUGH!
Why did I pretend to be a karate-kicking adventurer in the first place?!?

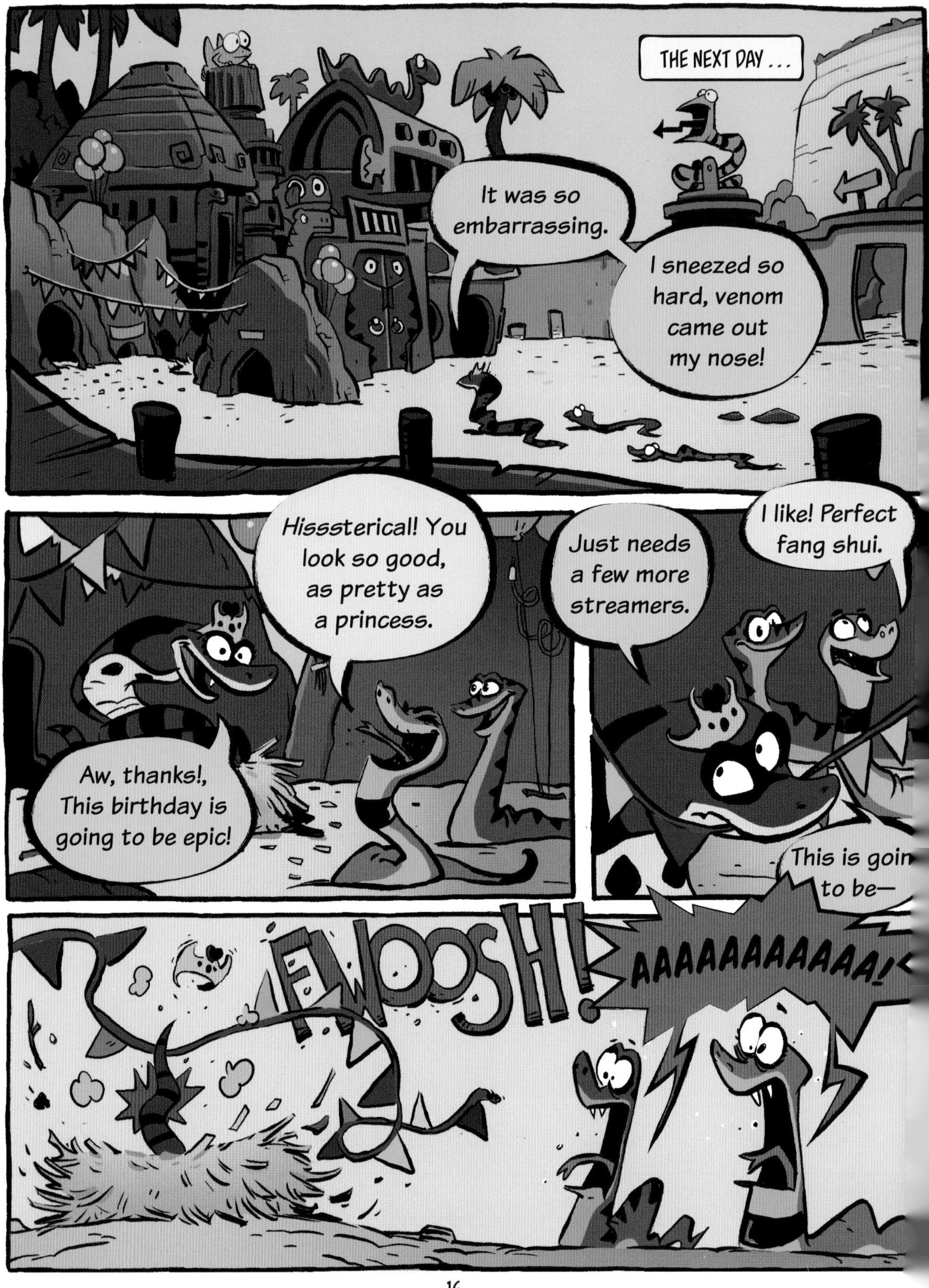
THE NEXT DAY . . .
It was so embarrassing.
I sneezed so hard, venom came out my nose!
Hisssterical! You look so good, as pretty as a princess.
Aw, thanks!, This birthday is going to be epic!
Just needs a few more streamers.
I like! Perfect fang shui.
This is goin to be—
FWOOSH!
AAAAAAAAAAA!

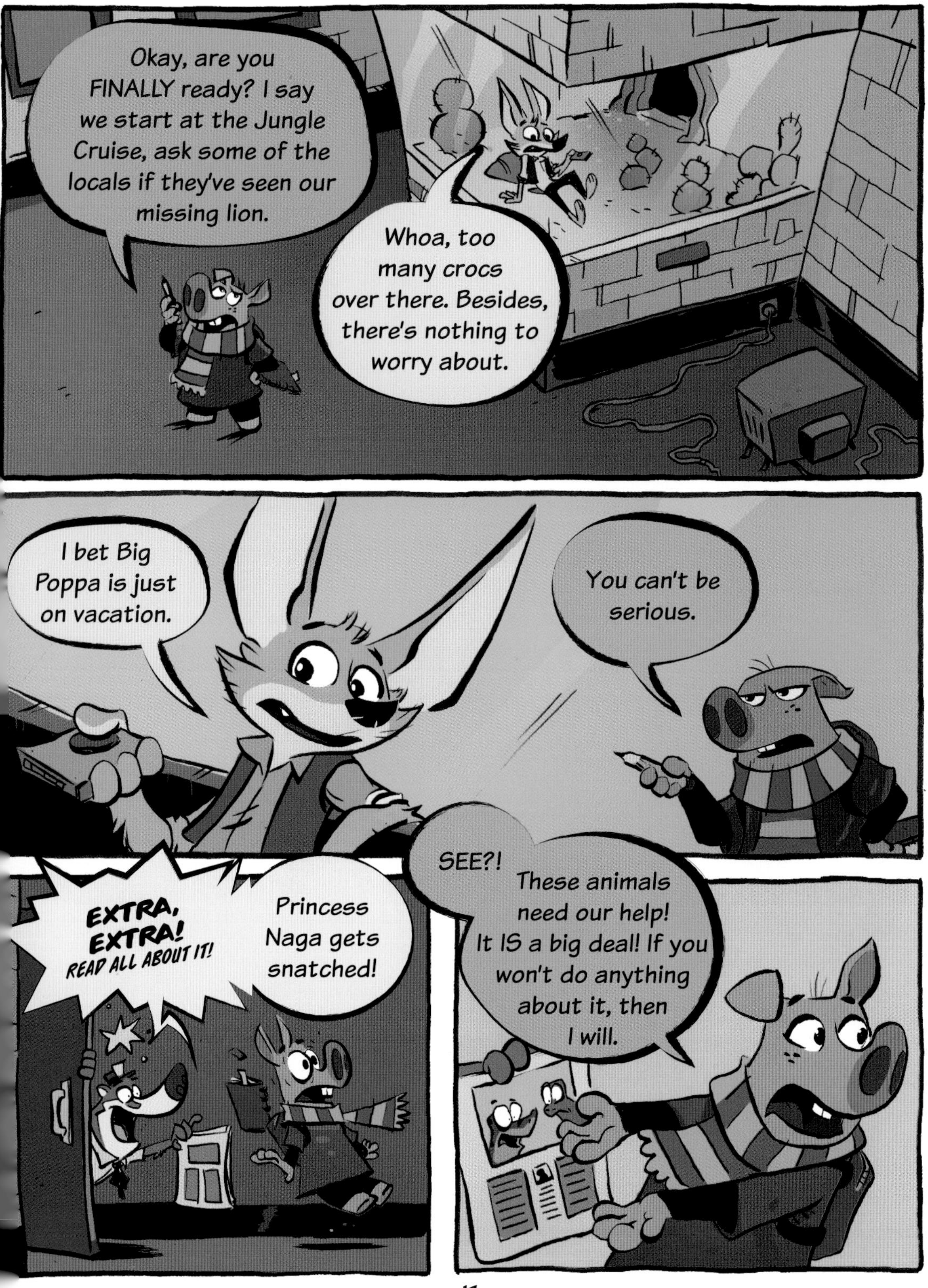
Okay, are you FINALLY ready? I say we start at the Jungle Cruise, ask some of the locals if they've seen our missing lion.
Whoa, too many crocs over there. Besides, there's nothing to worry about.
I bet Big Poppa is just on vacation.
You can't be serious.
EXTRA, EXTRA! READ ALL ABOUT IT!
Princess Naga gets snatched!
SEE?!
These animals need our help! It IS a big deal! If you won't do anything about it, then I will.

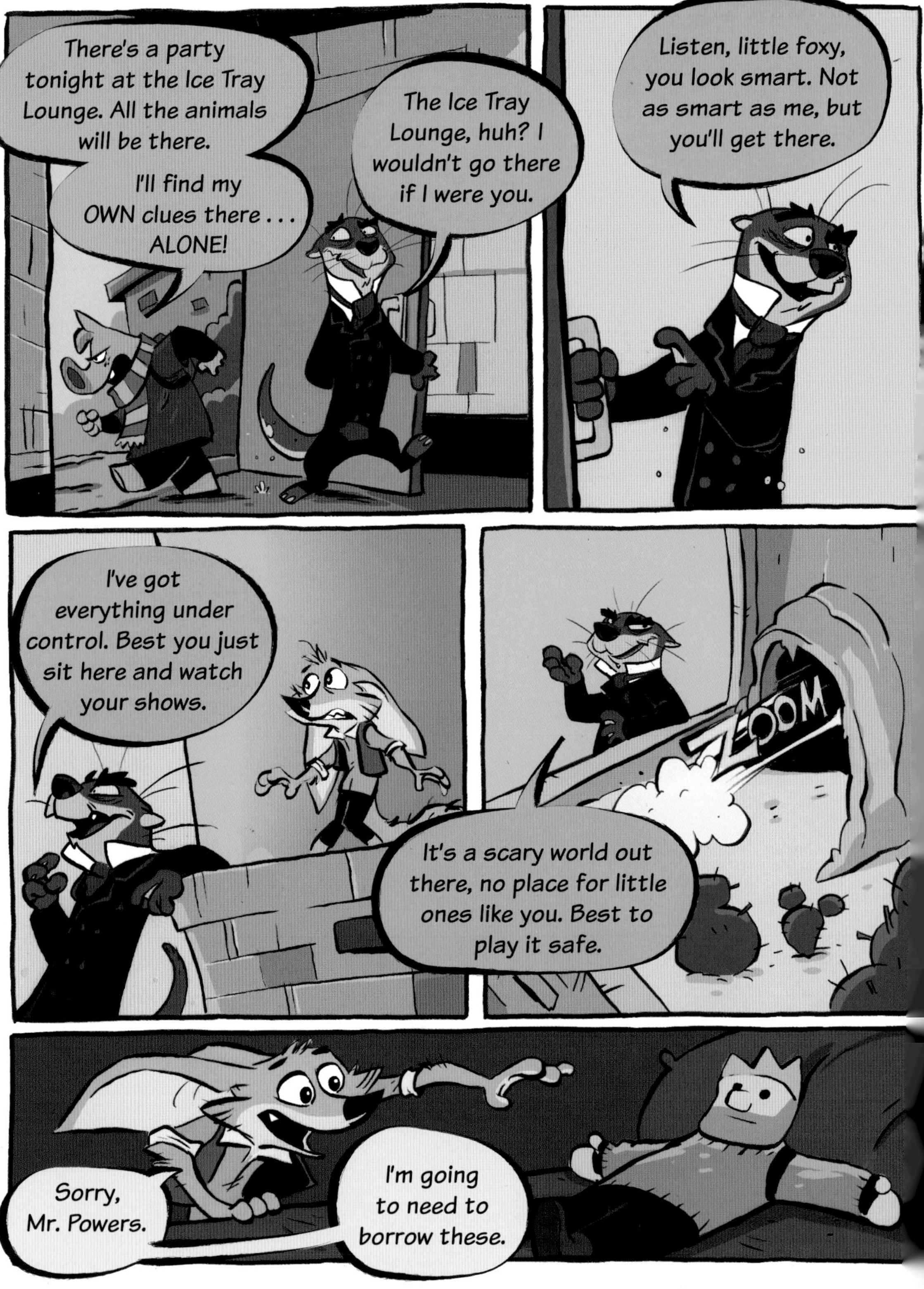
There's a party tonight at the Ice Tray Lounge. All the animals will be there.
I'll find my OWN clues there . . . ALONE!
The Ice Tray Lounge, huh? I wouldn't go there if I were you.
Listen, little foxy, you look smart. Not as smart as me, but you'll get there.
I've got everything under control. Best you just sit here and watch your shows.
ZOOM
It's a scary world out there, no place for little ones like you. Best to play it safe.
Sorry, Mr. Powers.
I'm going to need to borrow these.

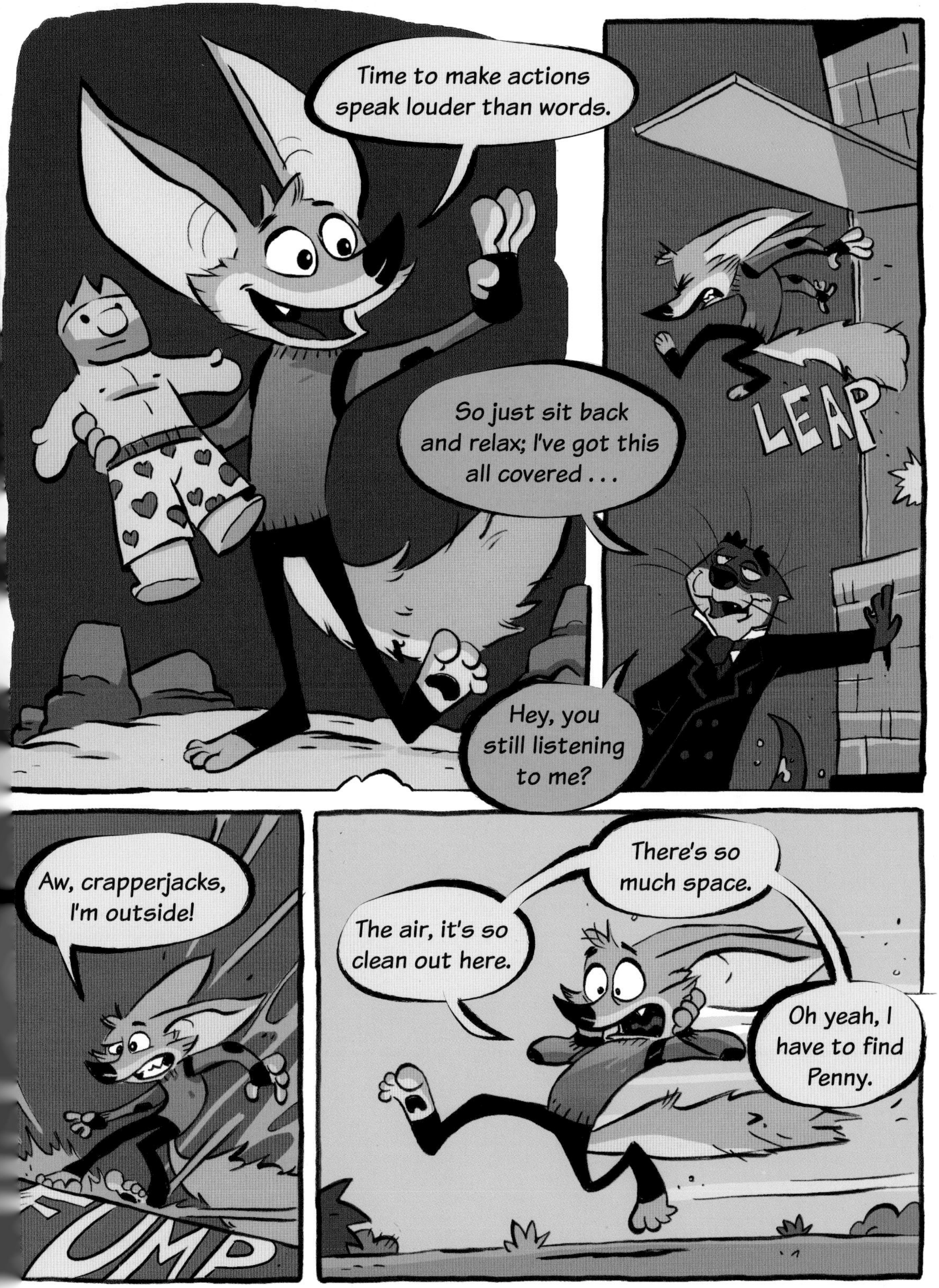
Time to make actions speak louder than words.
So just sit back and relax; I've got this all covered . . .
LEAP
Hey, you still listening to me?
Aw, crapperjacks, I'm outside!
THUMP
There's so much space.
The air, it's so clean out here.
Oh yeah, I have to find Penny.

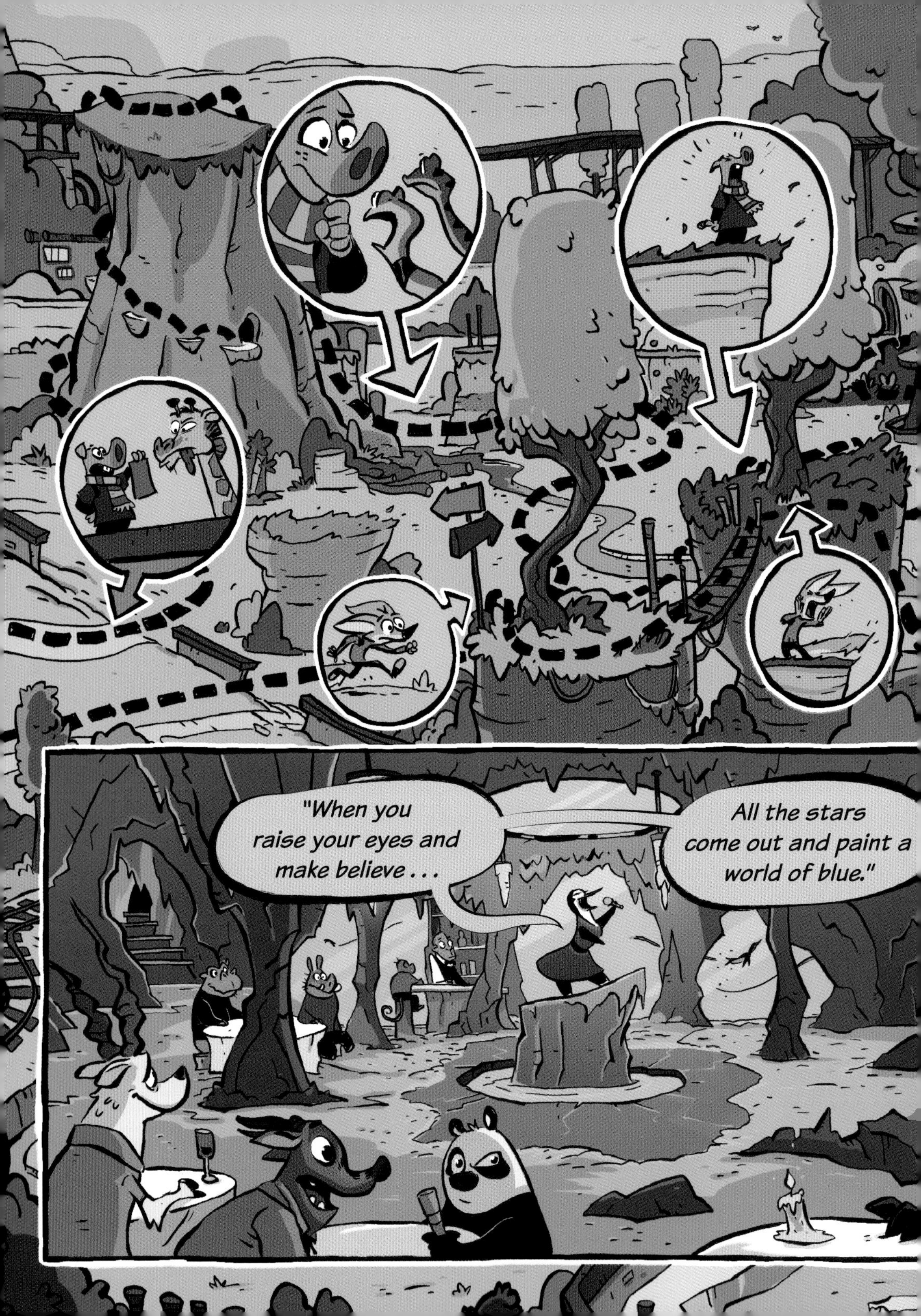
"When you raise your eyes and make believe . . .
All the stars come out and paint a world of blue."

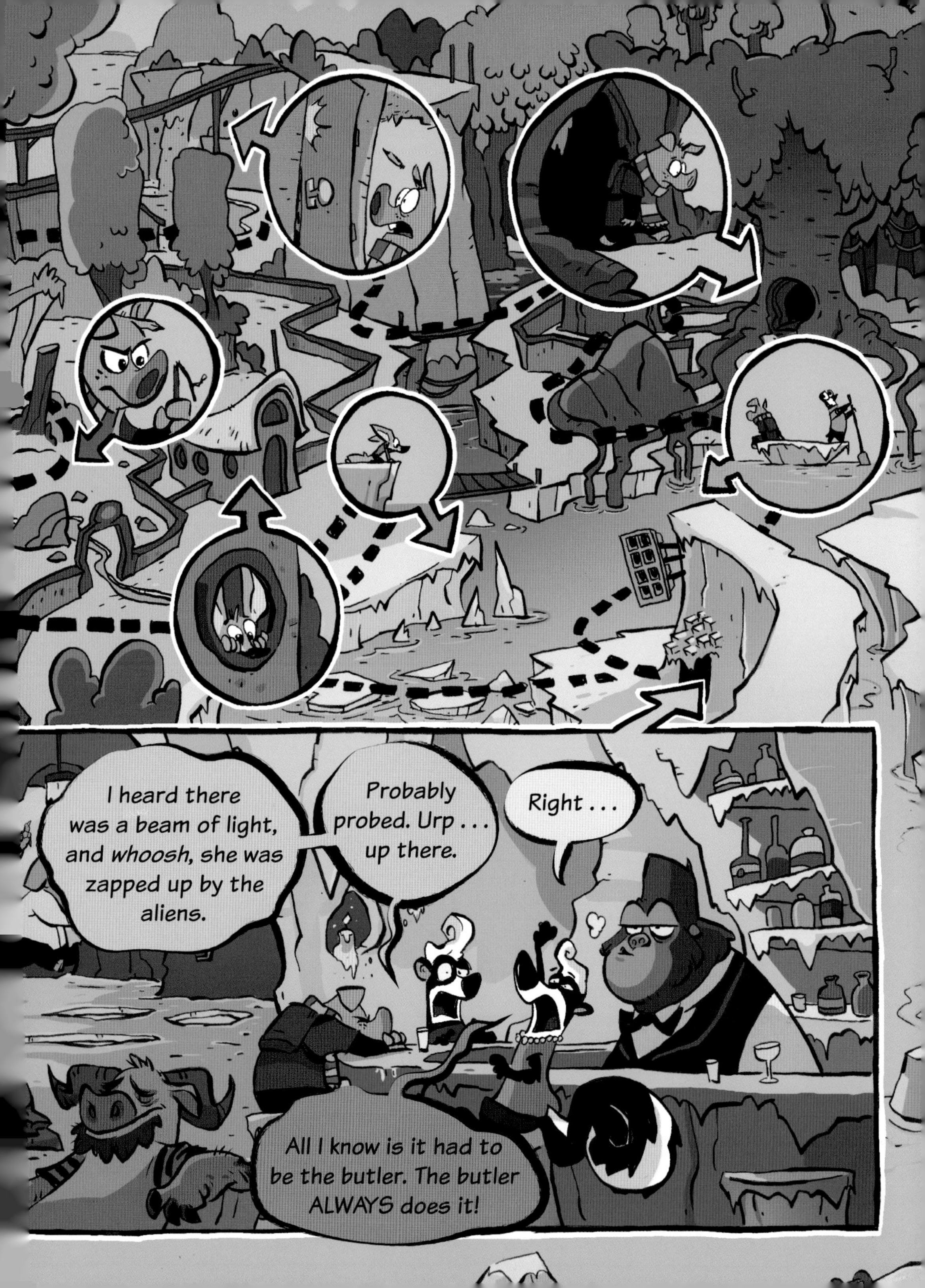
I heard there was a beam of light, and *whoosh*, she was zapped up by the aliens.
Probably probed. Urp . . . up there.
Right . . .
All I know is it had to be the butler. The butler ALWAYS does it!

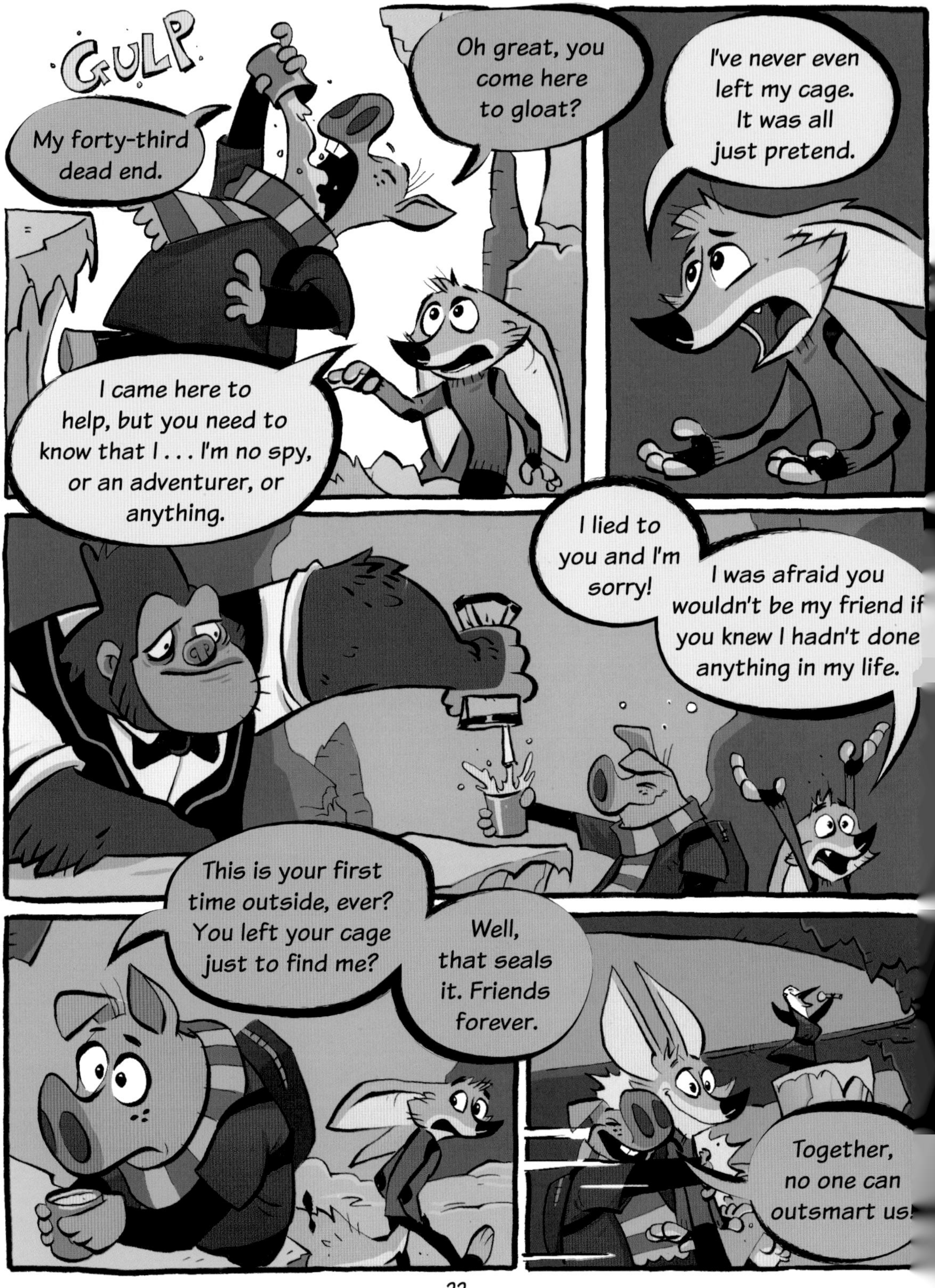
GULP
My forty-third dead end.
Oh great, you come here to gloat?
I came here to help, but you need to know that I . . . I'm no spy, or an adventurer, or anything.
I've never even left my cage. It was all just pretend.
I lied to you and I'm sorry!
I was afraid you wouldn't be my friend if you knew I hadn't done anything in my life.
This is your first time outside, ever? You left your cage just to find me?
Well, that seals it. Friends forever.
Together, no one can outsmart us!

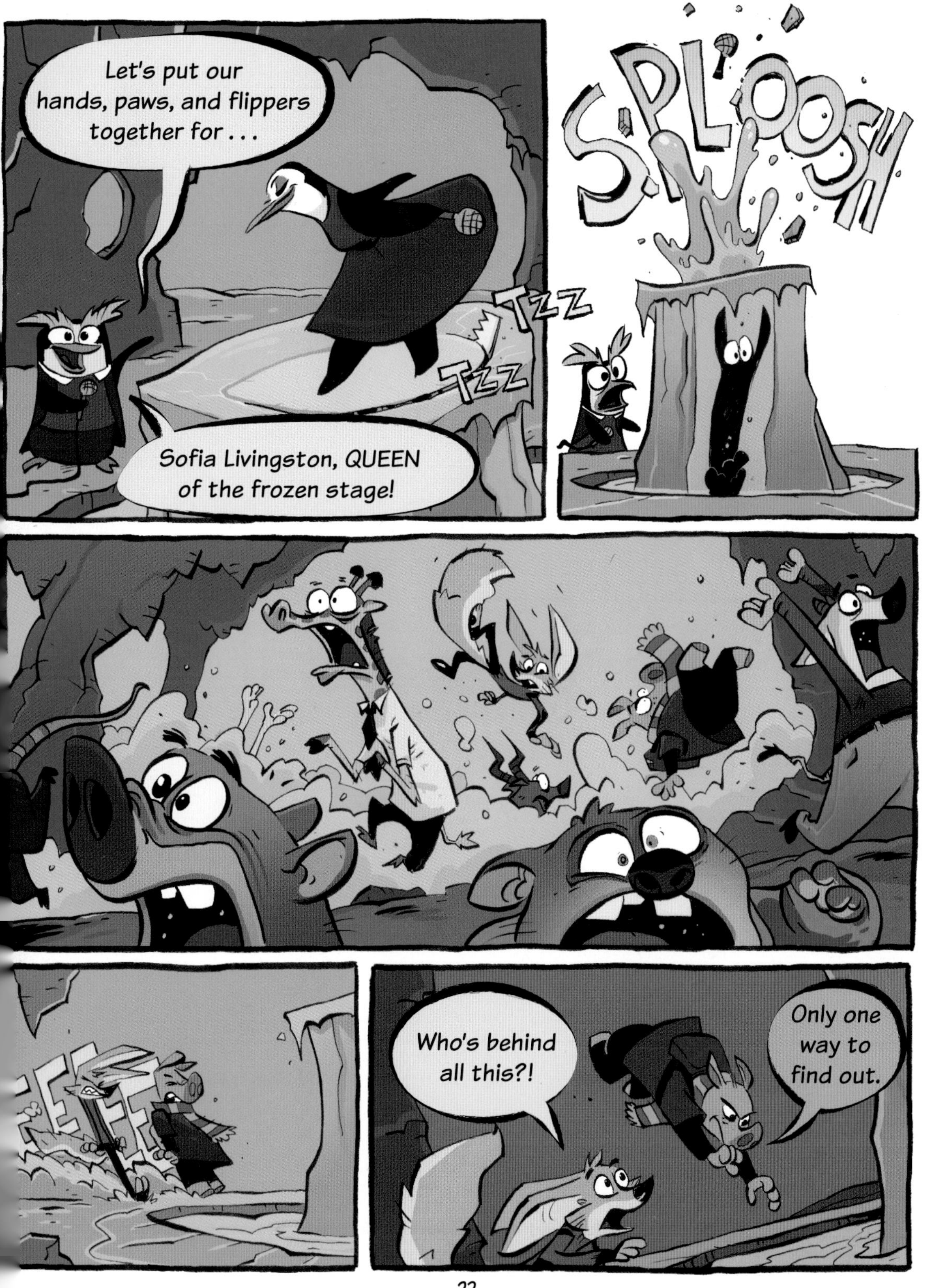
Let's put our hands, paws, and flippers together for . . .
TZZ
TZZ
Sofia Livingston, QUEEN of the frozen stage!
SPLOOSH
Who's behind all this?!
Only one way to find out.

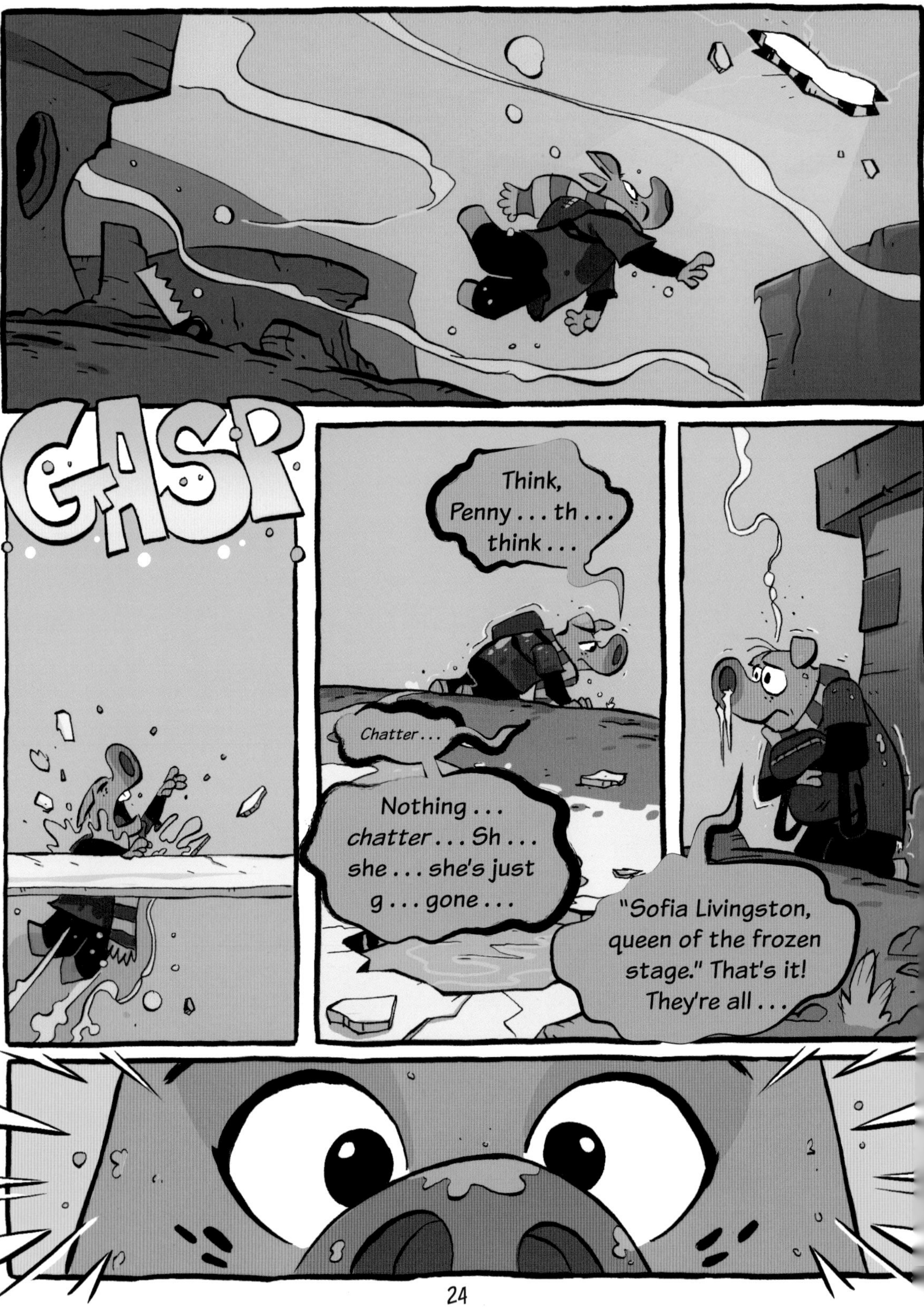
GASP
Think, Penny . . . th . . . think . . .
Chatter . . .
Nothing . . . chatter . . . Sh . . . she . . . she's just g . . . gone . . .
"Sofia Livingston, queen of the frozen stage." That's it! They're all . . .

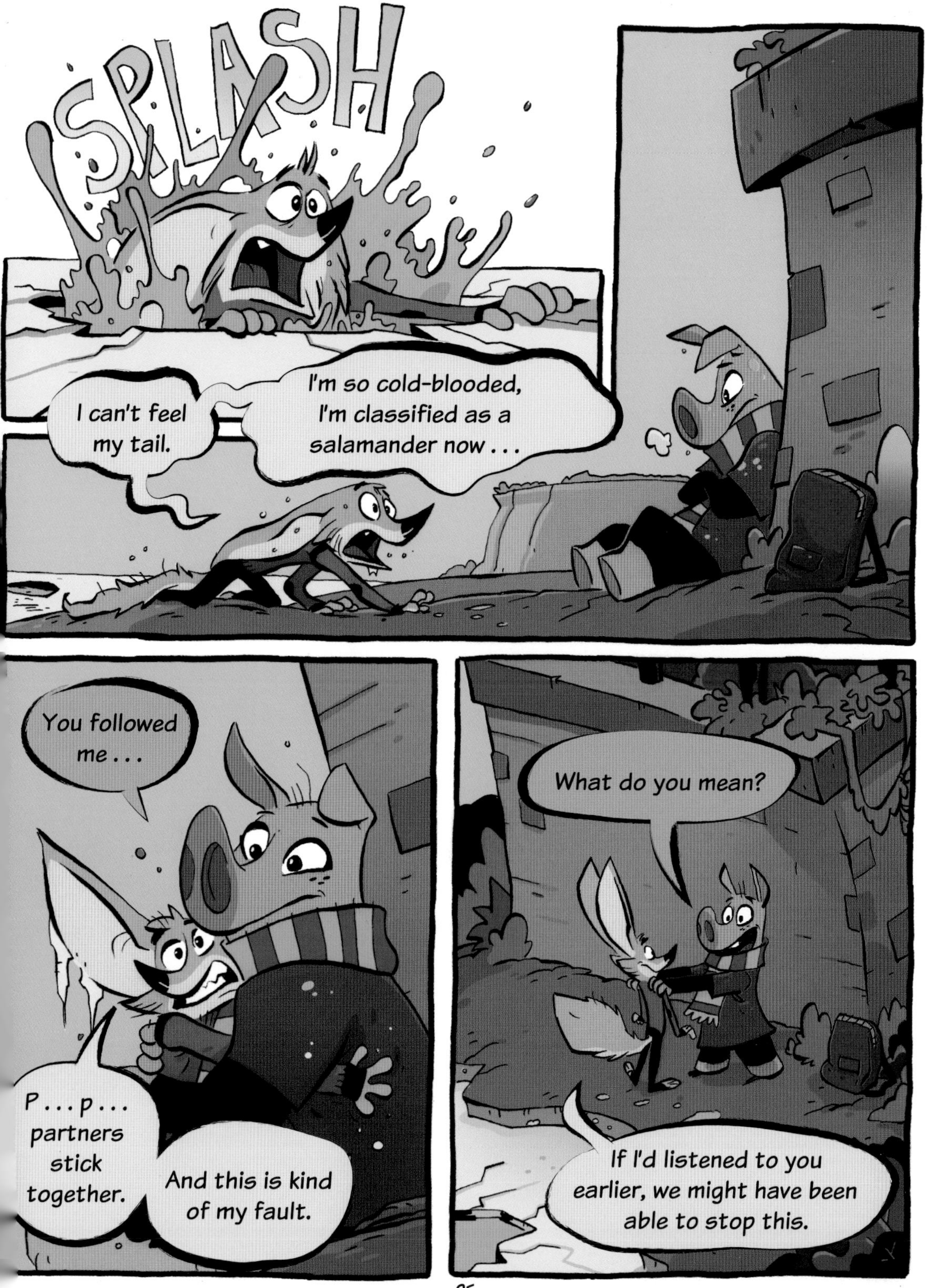
SPLASH
I can't feel my tail.
I'm so cold-blooded, I'm classified as a salamander now . . .
You followed me . . .
P . . . p . . . partners stick together.
And this is kind of my fault.
What do you mean?
If I'd listened to you earlier, we might have been able to stop this.

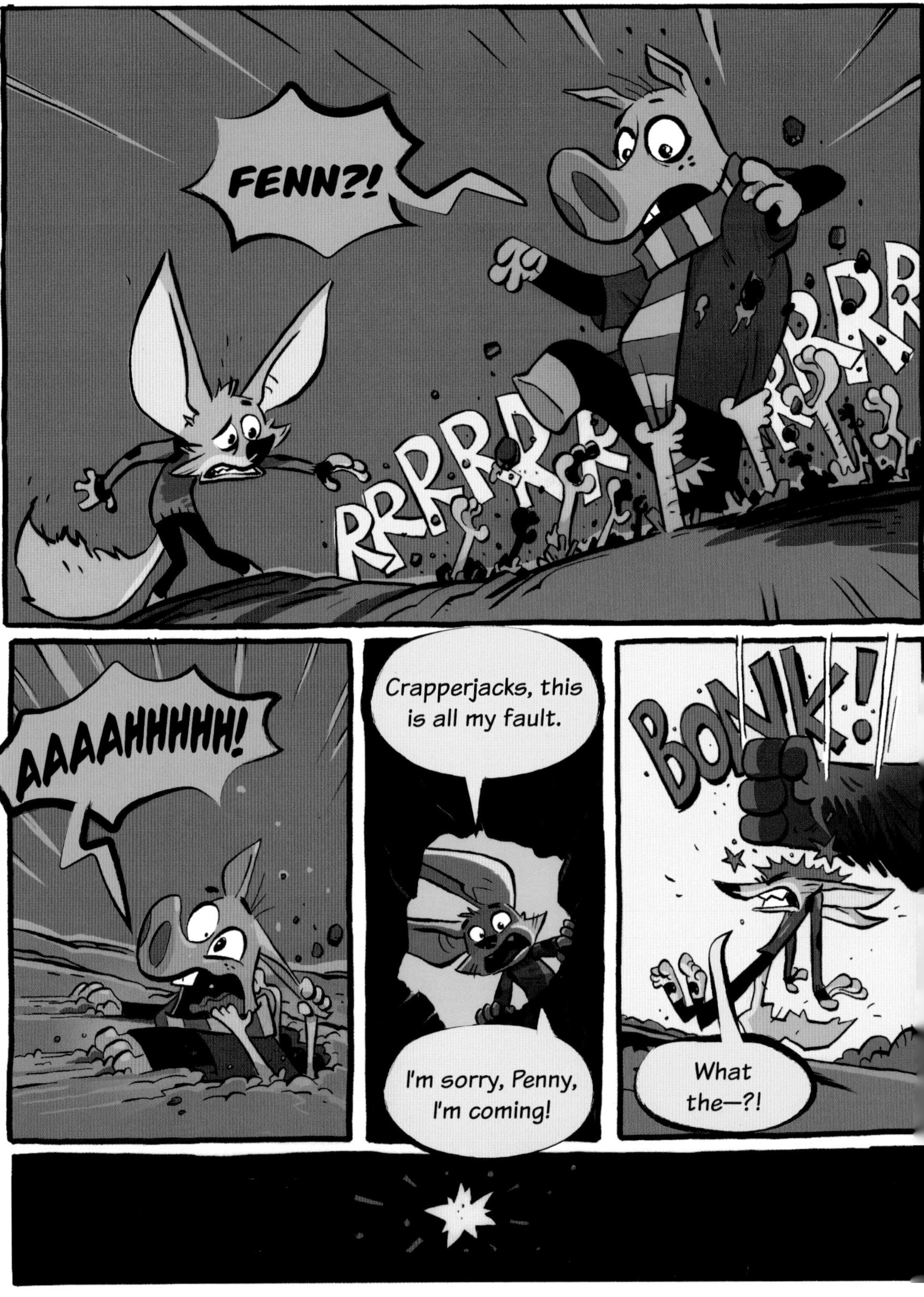
FENN?!
RRRRRRRRRRRRRR
AAAAHHHHH!
Crapperjacks, this is all my fault.
I'm sorry, Penny, I'm coming!
BONK!!
What the—?!

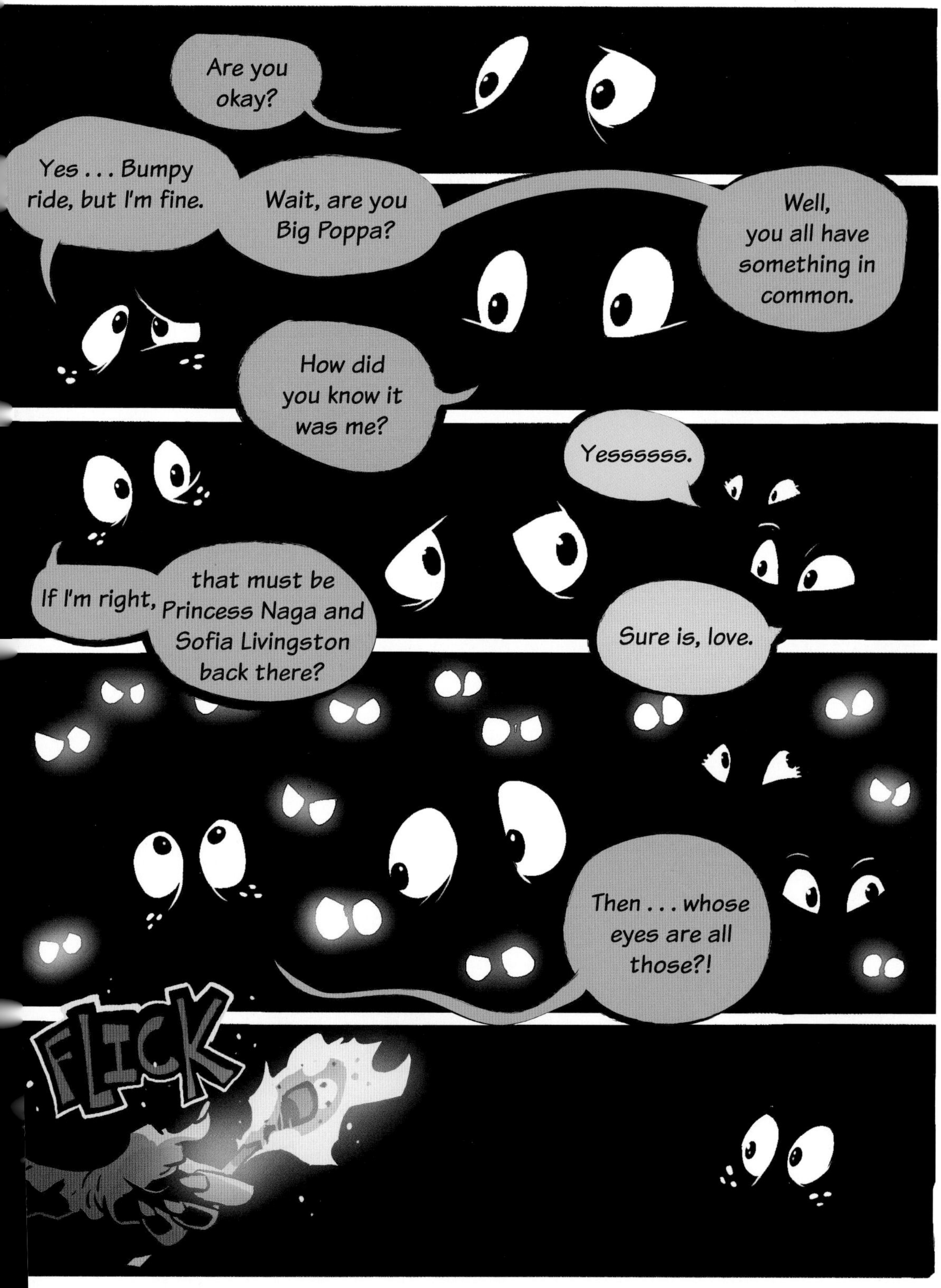
Are you okay?
Yes . . . Bumpy ride, but I'm fine.
Wait, are you Big Poppa?
Well, you all have something in common.
How did you know it was me?
Yessssss.
If I'm right,
that must be Princess Naga and Sofia Livingston back there?
Sure is, love.
Then . . . whose eyes are all those?!
FLICK

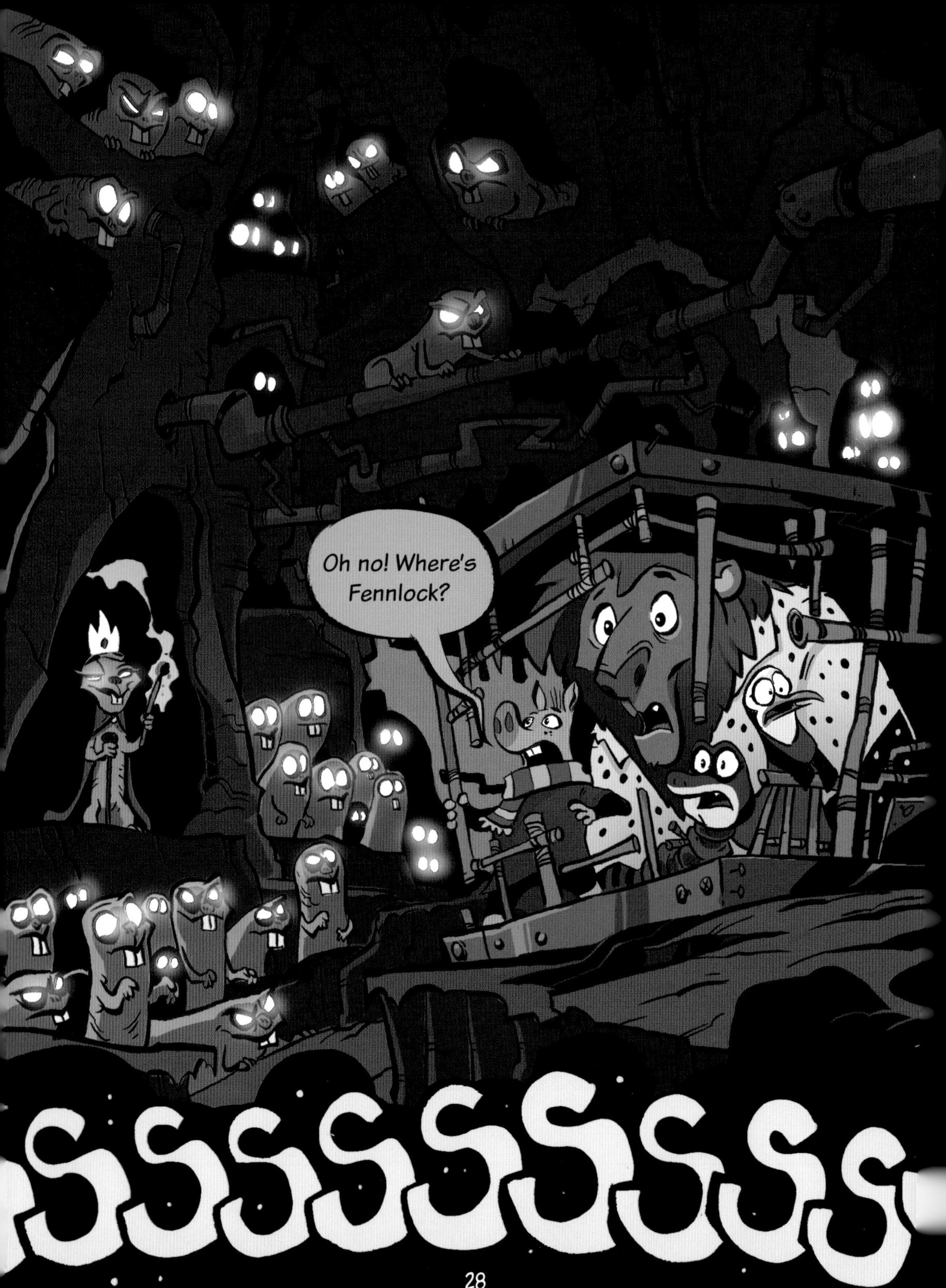
Oh no! Where's Fennlock?
SSSSSSSSS

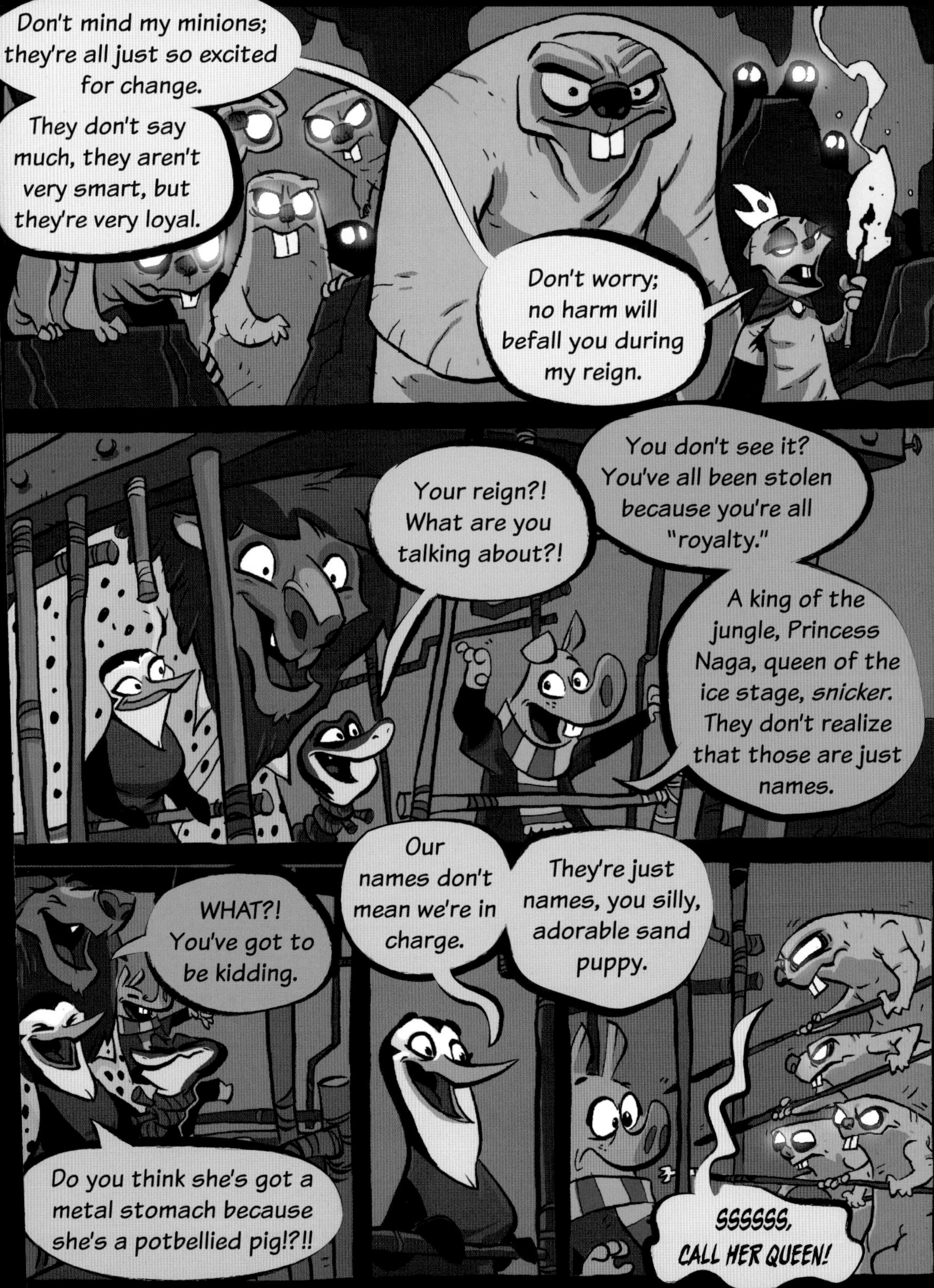

Don't mind my minions; they're all just so excited for change.
They don't say much, they aren't very smart, but they're very loyal.
Don't worry; no harm will befall you during my reign.
Your reign?! What are you talking about?!
You don't see it? You've all been stolen because you're all "royalty."
A king of the jungle, Princess Naga, queen of the ice stage, snicker. They don't realize that those are just names.
WHAT?! You've got to be kidding.
Our names don't mean we're in charge.
They're just names, you silly, adorable sand puppy.
Do you think she's got a metal stomach because she's a potbellied pig!?!!
SSSSSS, CALL HER QUEEN!

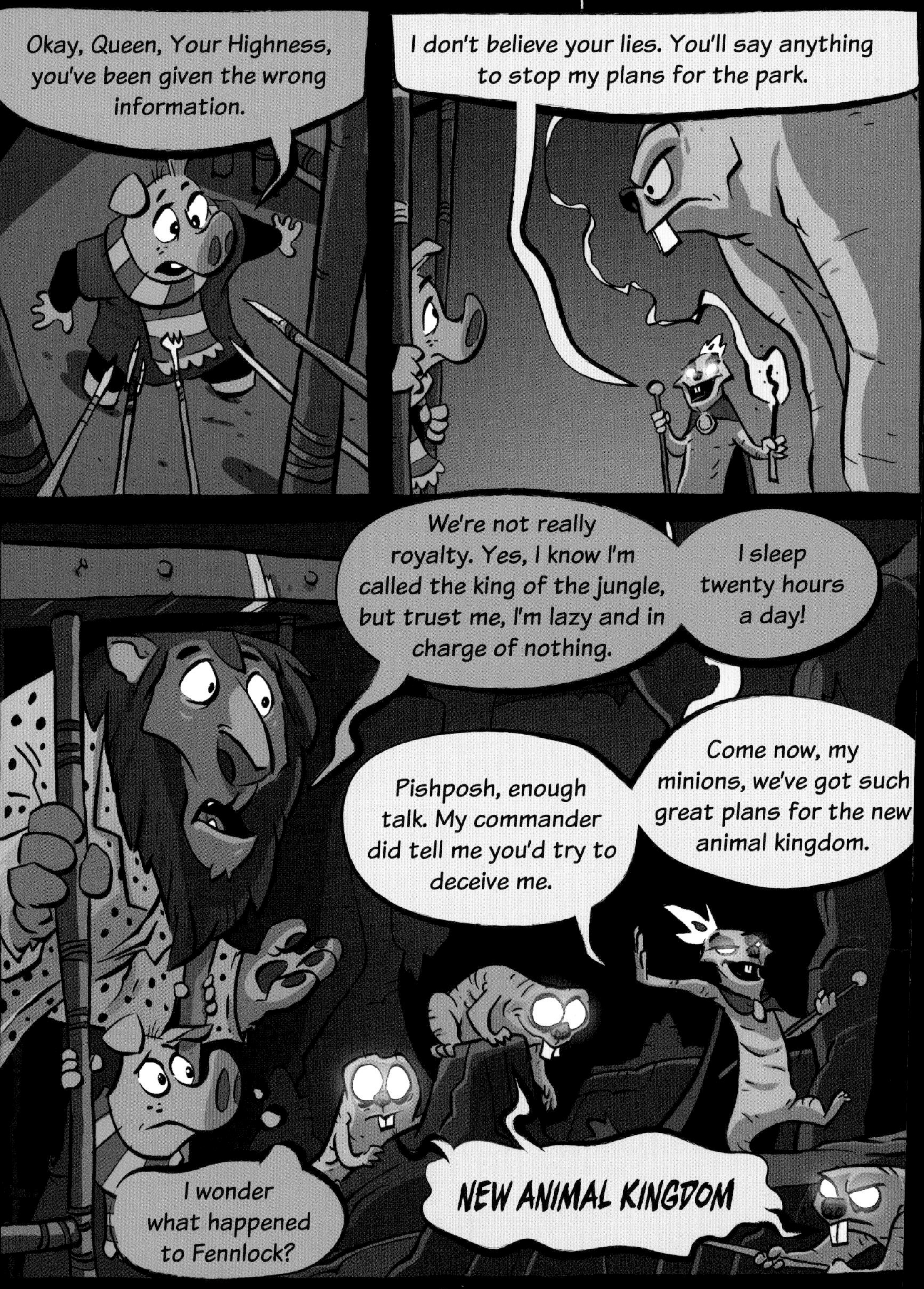
Okay, Queen, Your Highness, you've been given the wrong information.
I don't believe your lies. You'll say anything to stop my plans for the park.
We're not really royalty. Yes, I know I'm called the king of the jungle, but trust me, I'm lazy and in charge of nothing.
I sleep twenty hours a day!
Pishposh, enough talk. My commander did tell me you'd try to deceive me.
Come now, my minions, we've got such great plans for the new animal kingdom.
I wonder what happened to Fennlock?
NEW ANIMAL KINGDOM

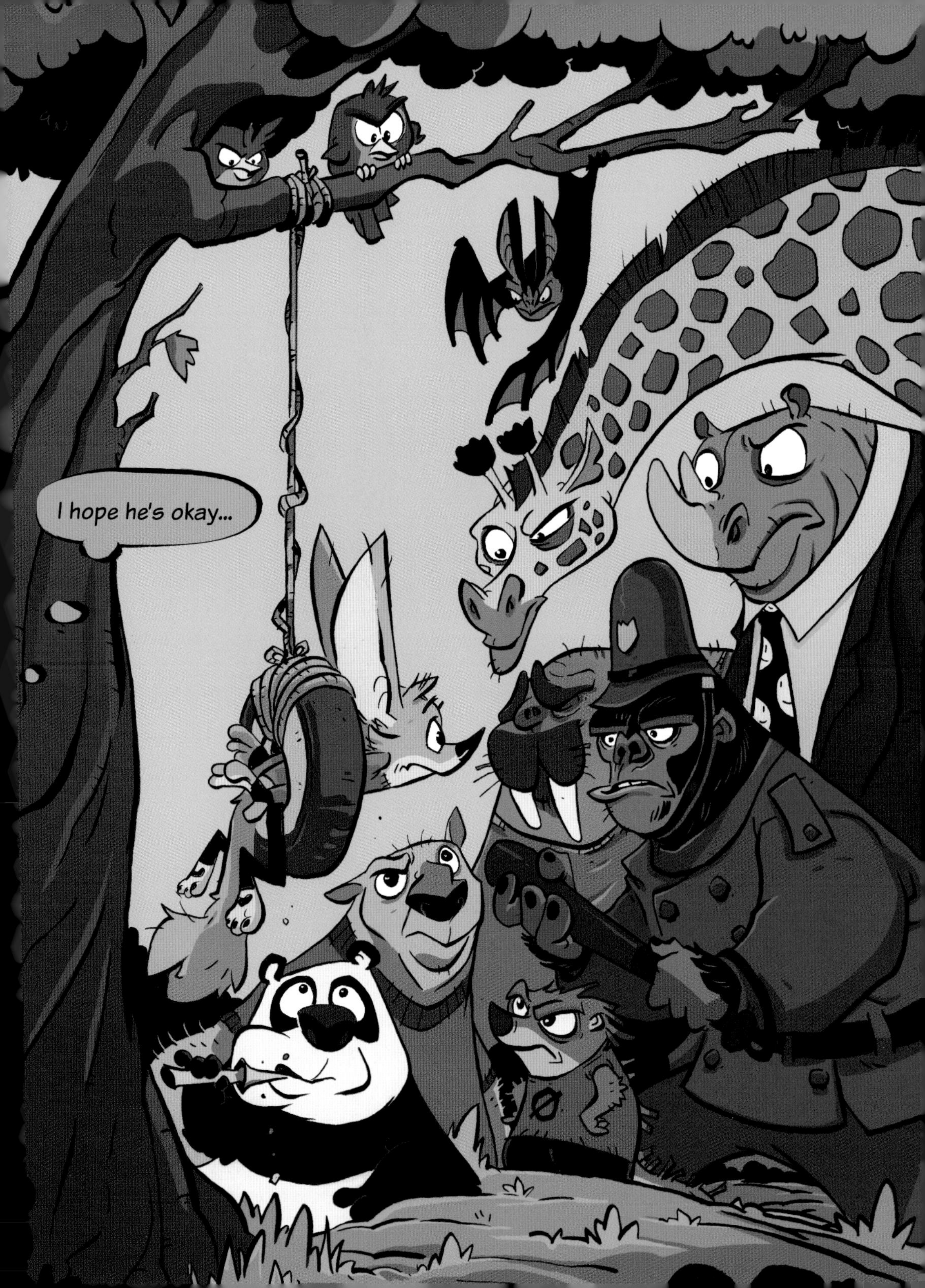
I hope he's okay...

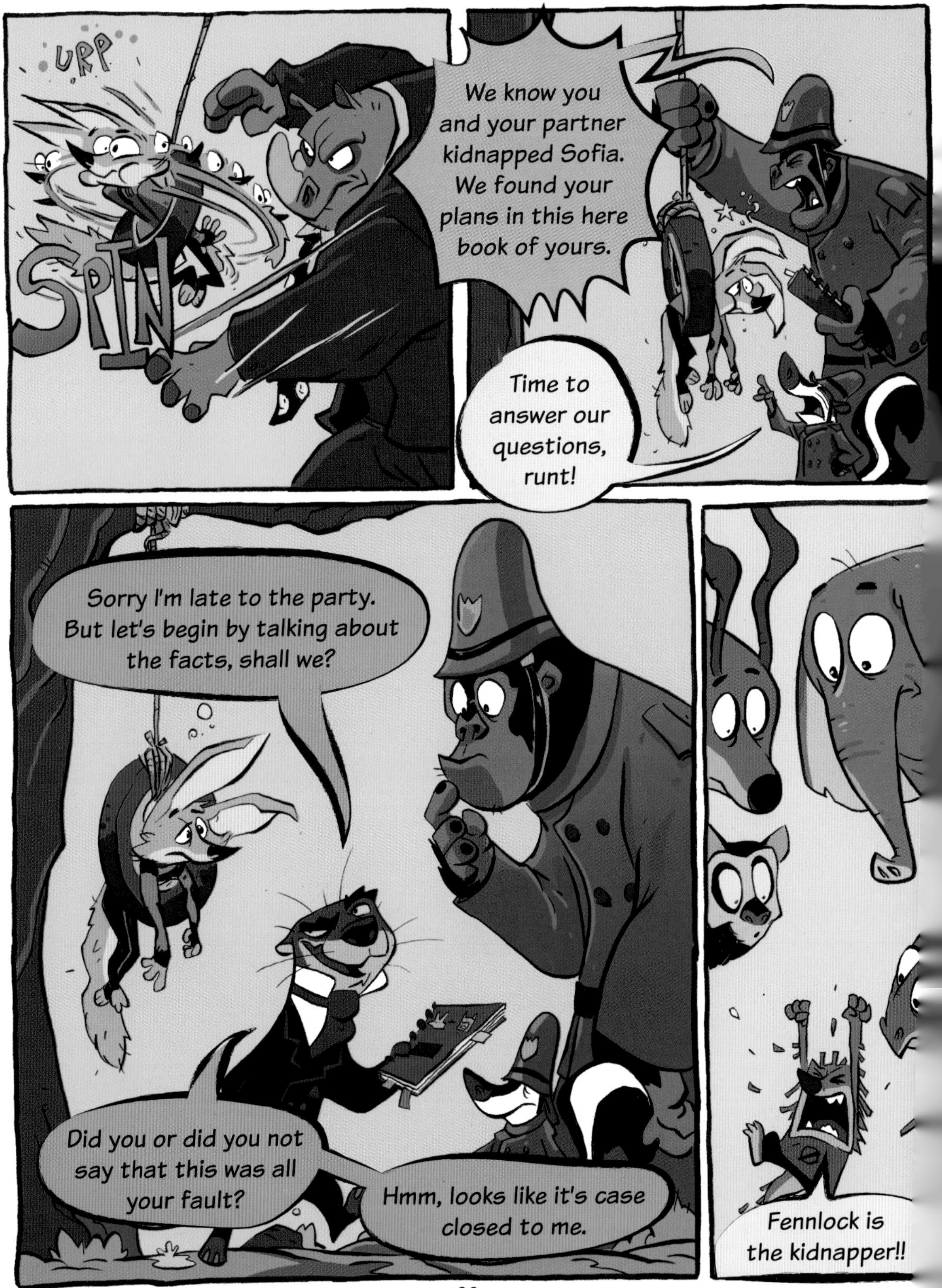
URP
SPIN
We know you and your partner kidnapped Sofia. We found your plans in this here book of yours.
Time to answer our questions, runt!
Sorry I'm late to the party. But let's begin by talking about the facts, shall we?
Did you or did you not say that this was all your fault?
Hmm, looks like it's case closed to me.
Fennlock is the kidnapper!!

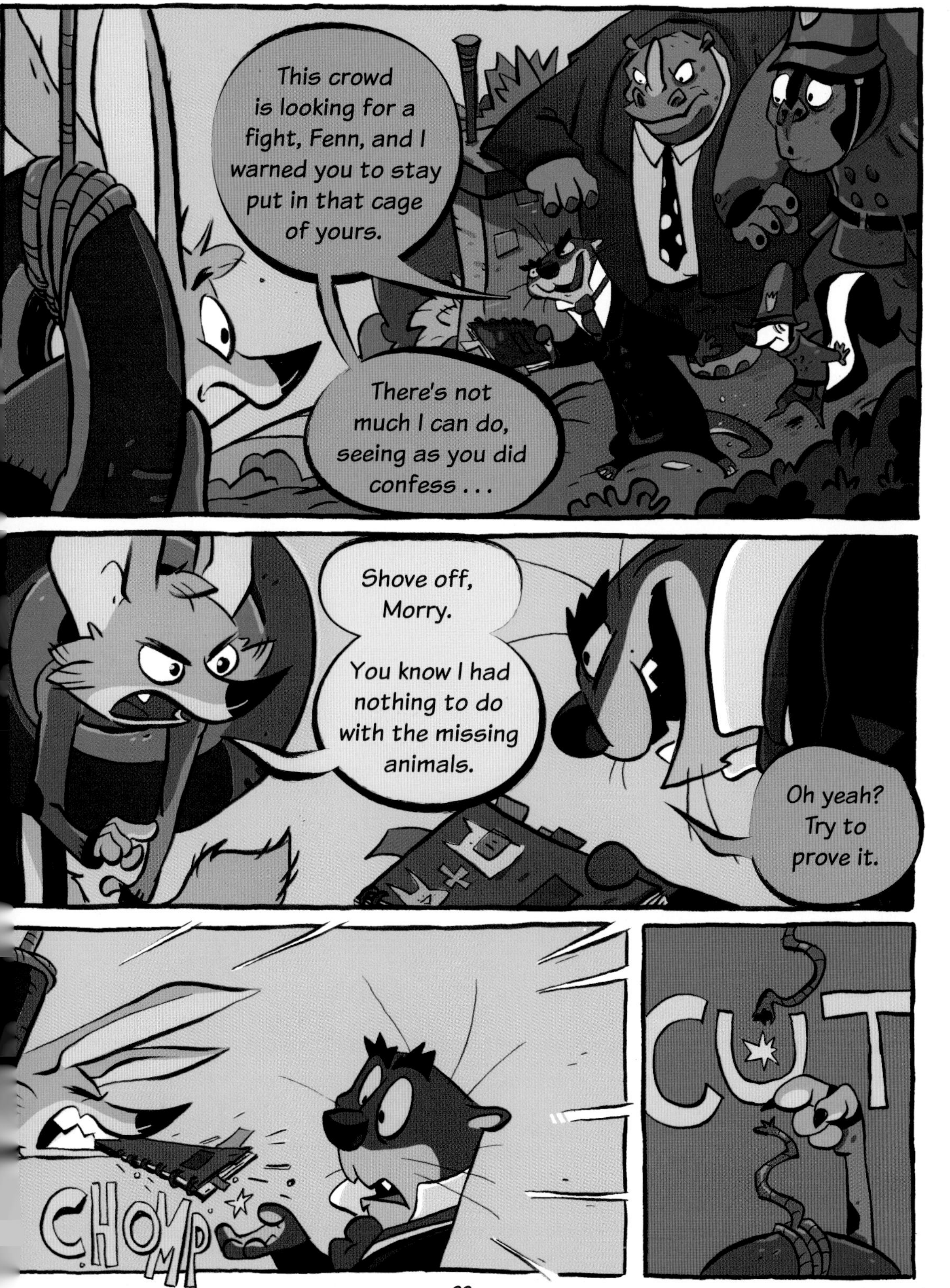
This crowd is looking for a fight, Fenn, and I warned you to stay put in that cage of yours.
There's not much I can do, seeing as you did confess . . .
Shove off, Morry.
You know I had nothing to do with the missing animals.
Oh yeah? Try to prove it.
CHOMP
CUT

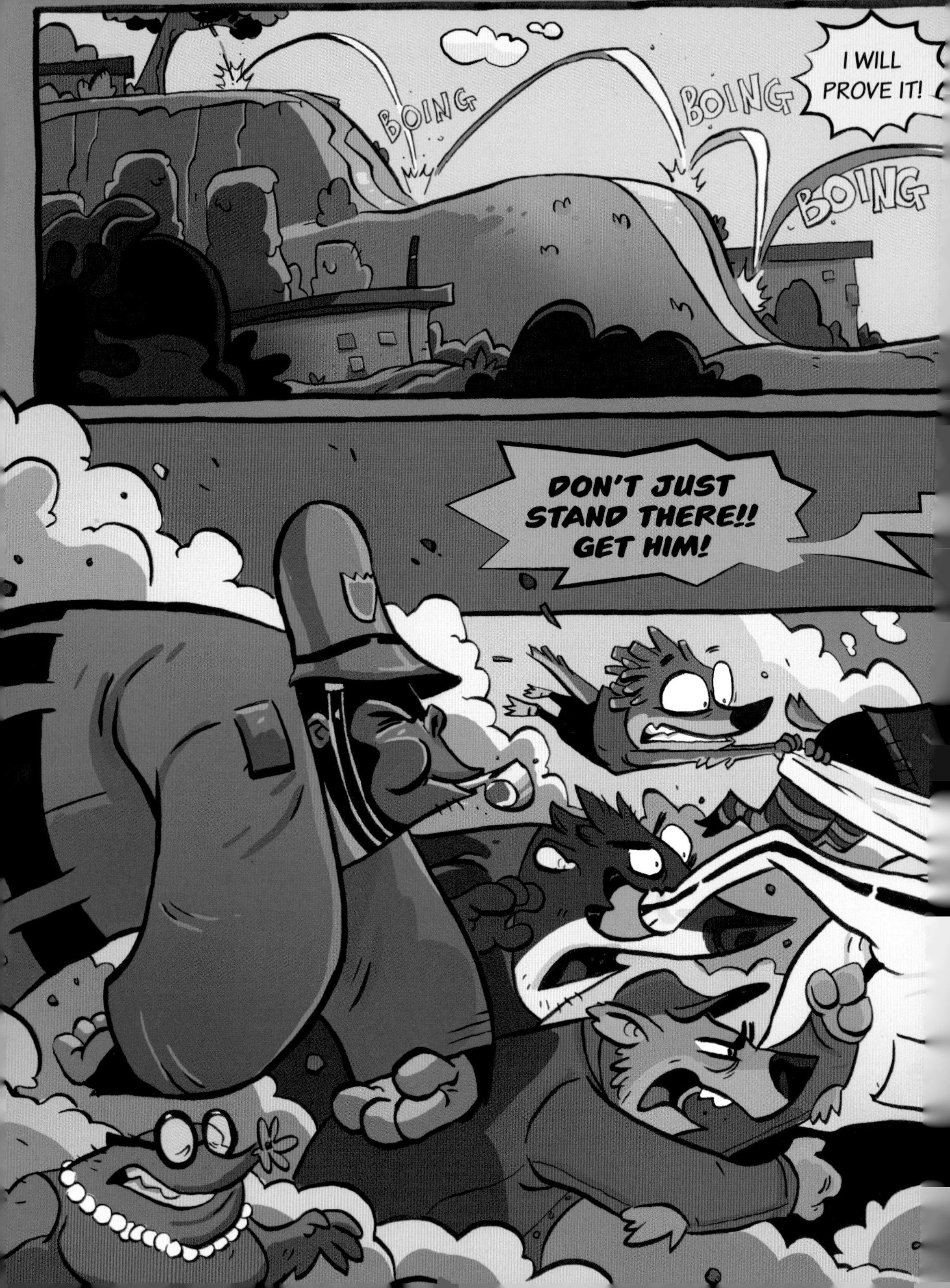
BOING
BOING
I WILL PROVE IT!
BOING
DON'T JUST STAND THERE!! GET HIM!

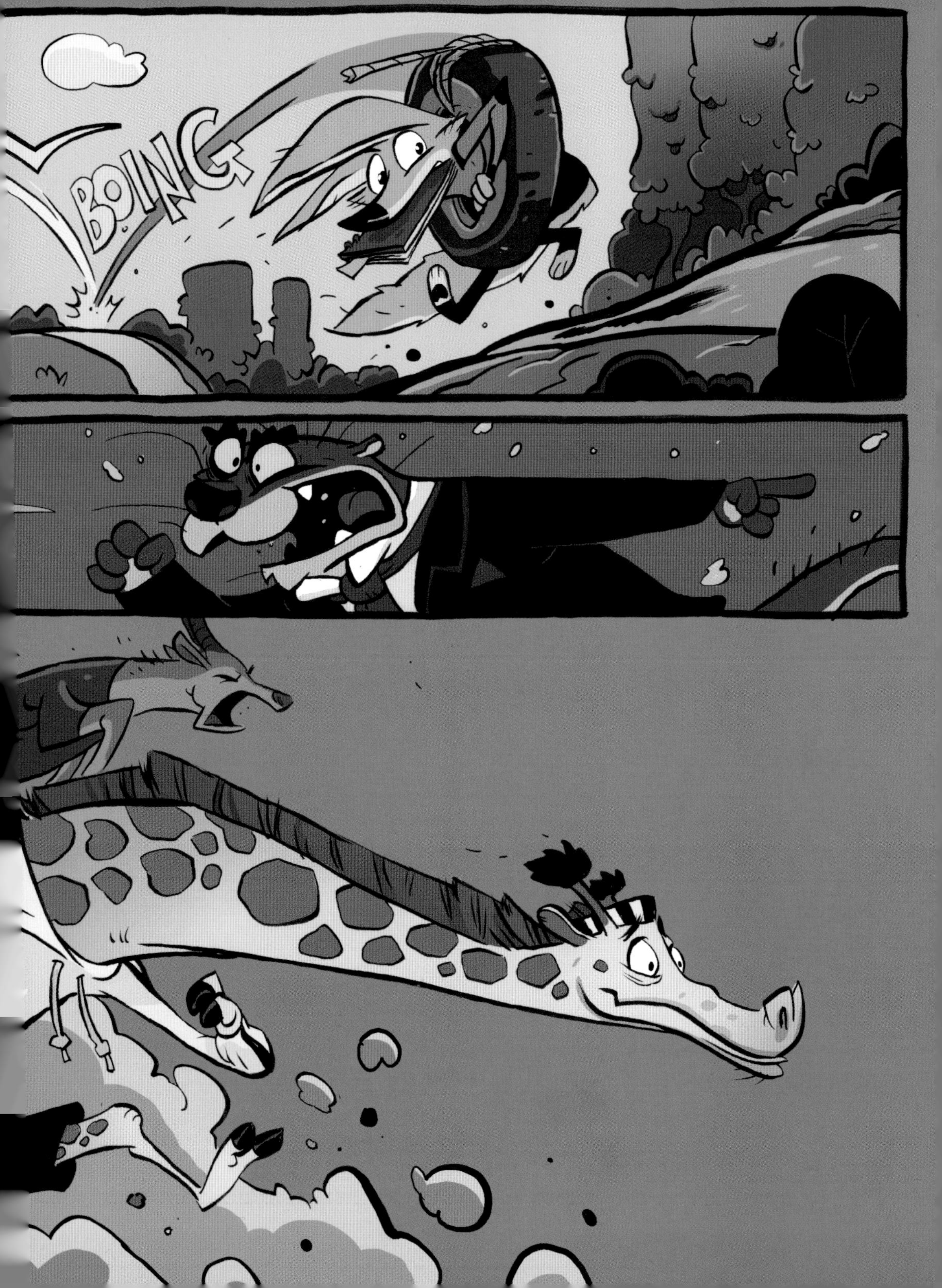
BOING

How am I going to find Penny . . . and prove I didn't do it?!

I'm no detective.

Hmmm . . . what would Penny do?

She'd probably make a list.

Poor little princess,

big ol' king of the jungle,

and the most beautiful singing queen in the animal kingdom . . .

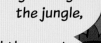

SKCH
SKcH
SKCH

I got it!

Maybe I am a detective after all!

I better get to the aquarium before the kidnapper!

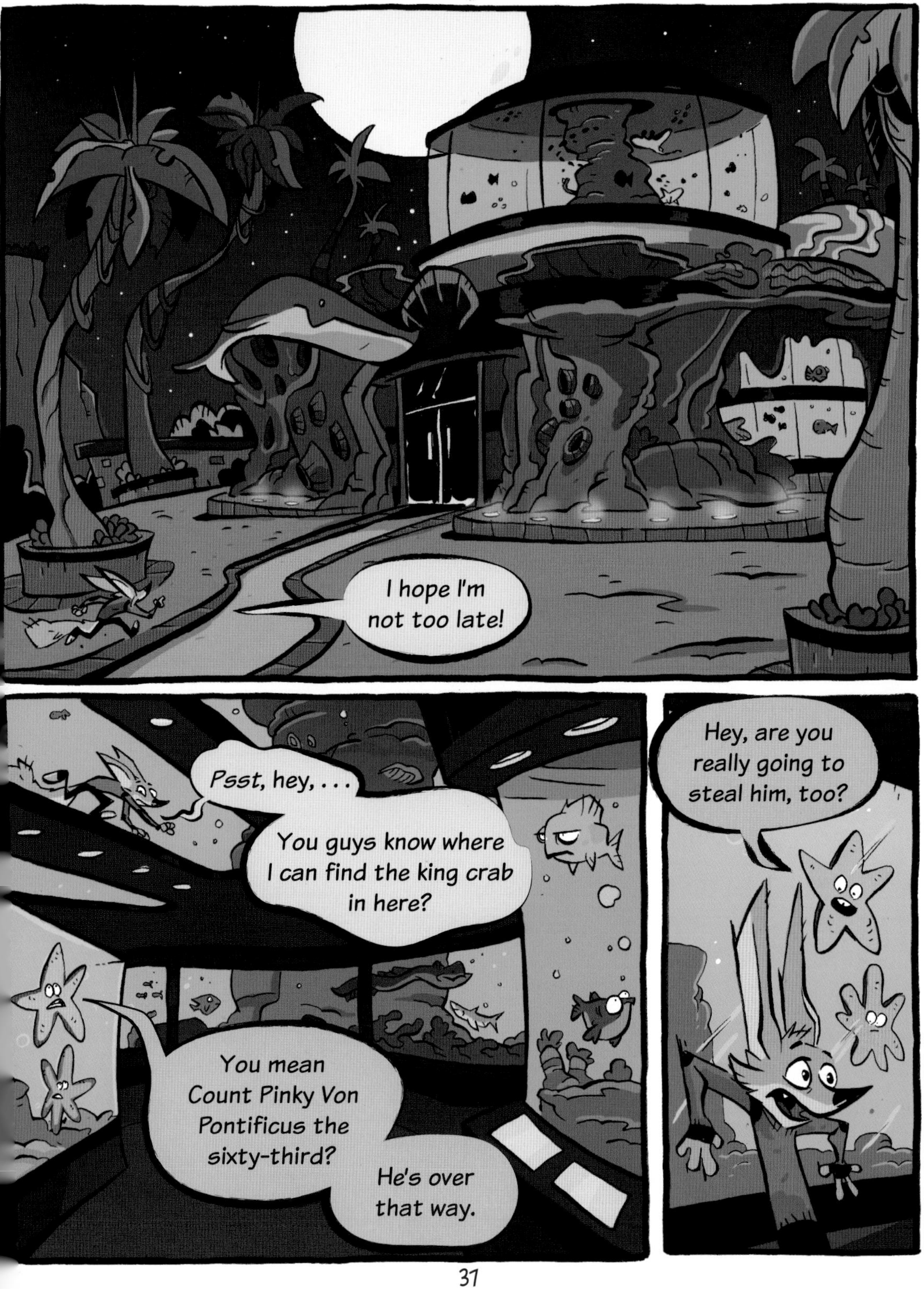
I hope I'm not too late!
Psst, hey, . . .
You guys know where I can find the king crab in here?
You mean Count Pinky Von Pontificus the sixty-third?
He's over that way.
Hey, are you really going to steal him, too?

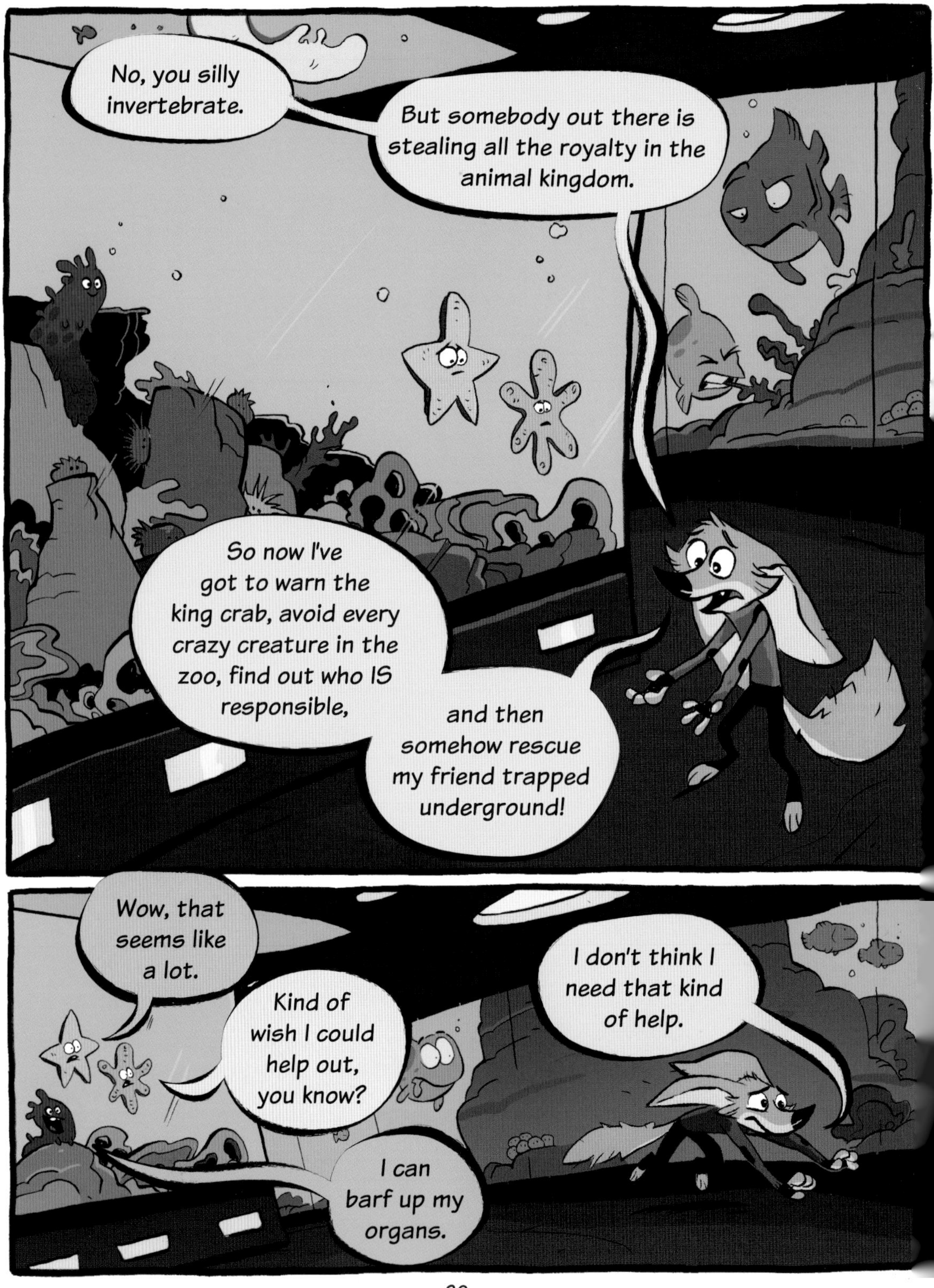
No, you silly invertebrate.
But somebody out there is stealing all the royalty in the animal kingdom.
So now I've got to warn the king crab, avoid every crazy creature in the zoo, find out who IS responsible,
and then somehow rescue my friend trapped underground!
Wow, that seems like a lot.
Kind of wish I could help out, you know?
I can barf up my organs.
I don't think I need that kind of help.

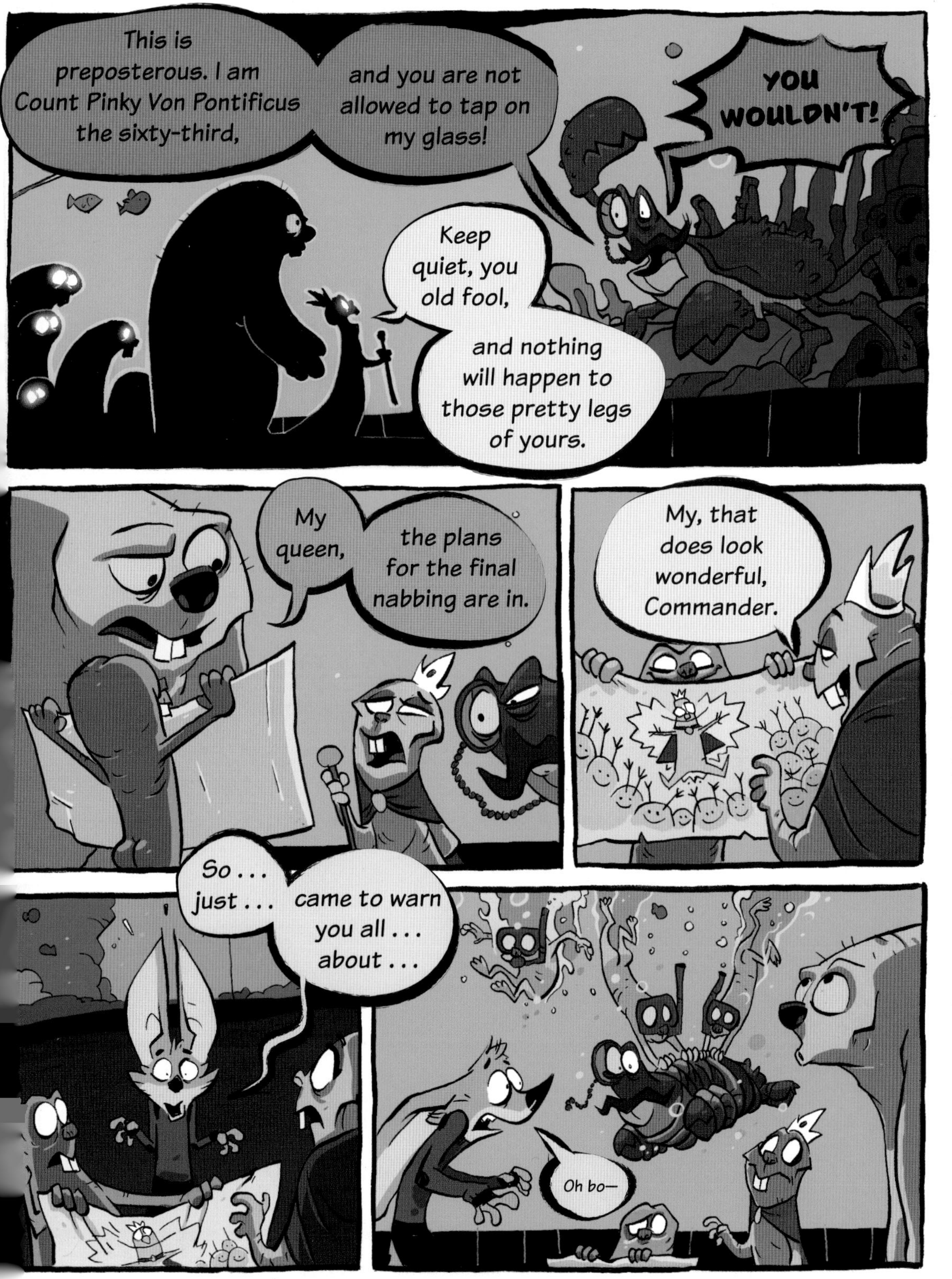
This is preposterous. I am Count Pinky Von Pontificus the sixty-third,
and you are not allowed to tap on my glass!
YOU WOULDN'T!
Keep quiet, you old fool,
and nothing will happen to those pretty legs of yours.
My queen,
the plans for the final nabbing are in.
My, that does look wonderful, Commander.
So . . . just . . .
came to warn you all . . . about . . .
Oh bo—

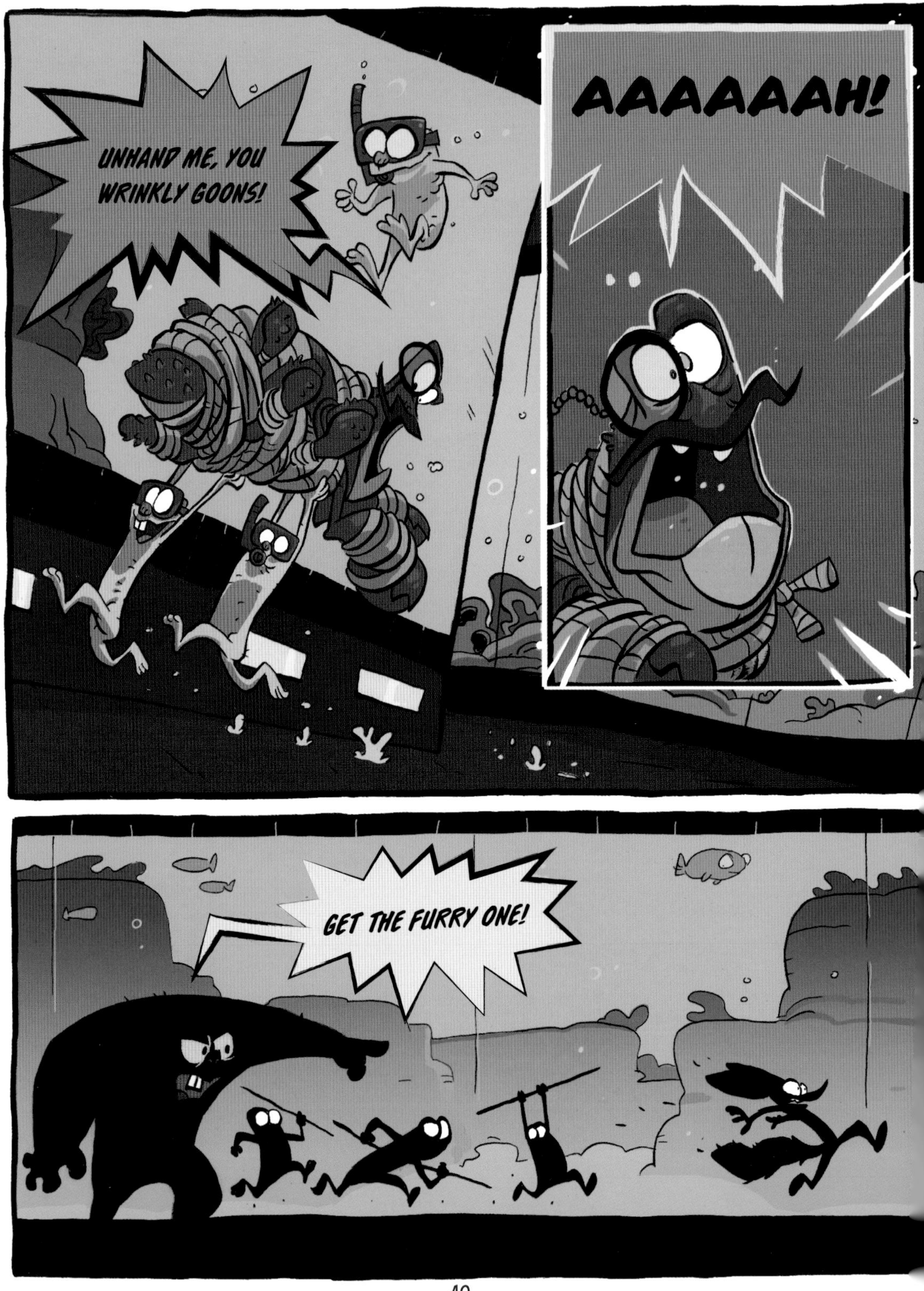
UNHAND ME, YOU WRINKLY GOONS!
AAAAAAH!
GET THE FURRY ONE!

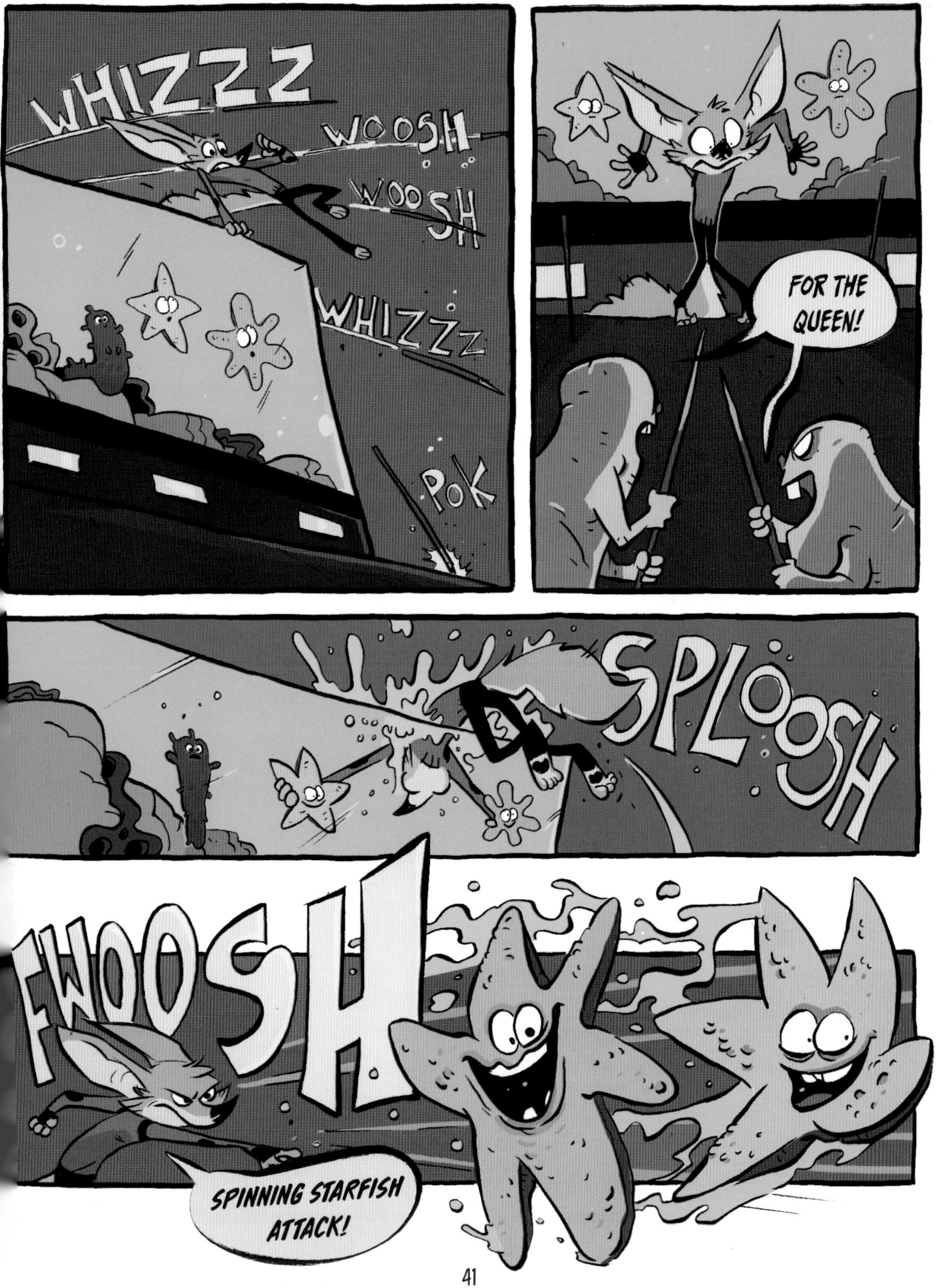
WHIZZZ
WOOSH
WOOSH
WHIZZz
POK
FOR THE QUEEN!
SPLOOSH
FWOOSH
SPINNING STARFISH ATTACK!

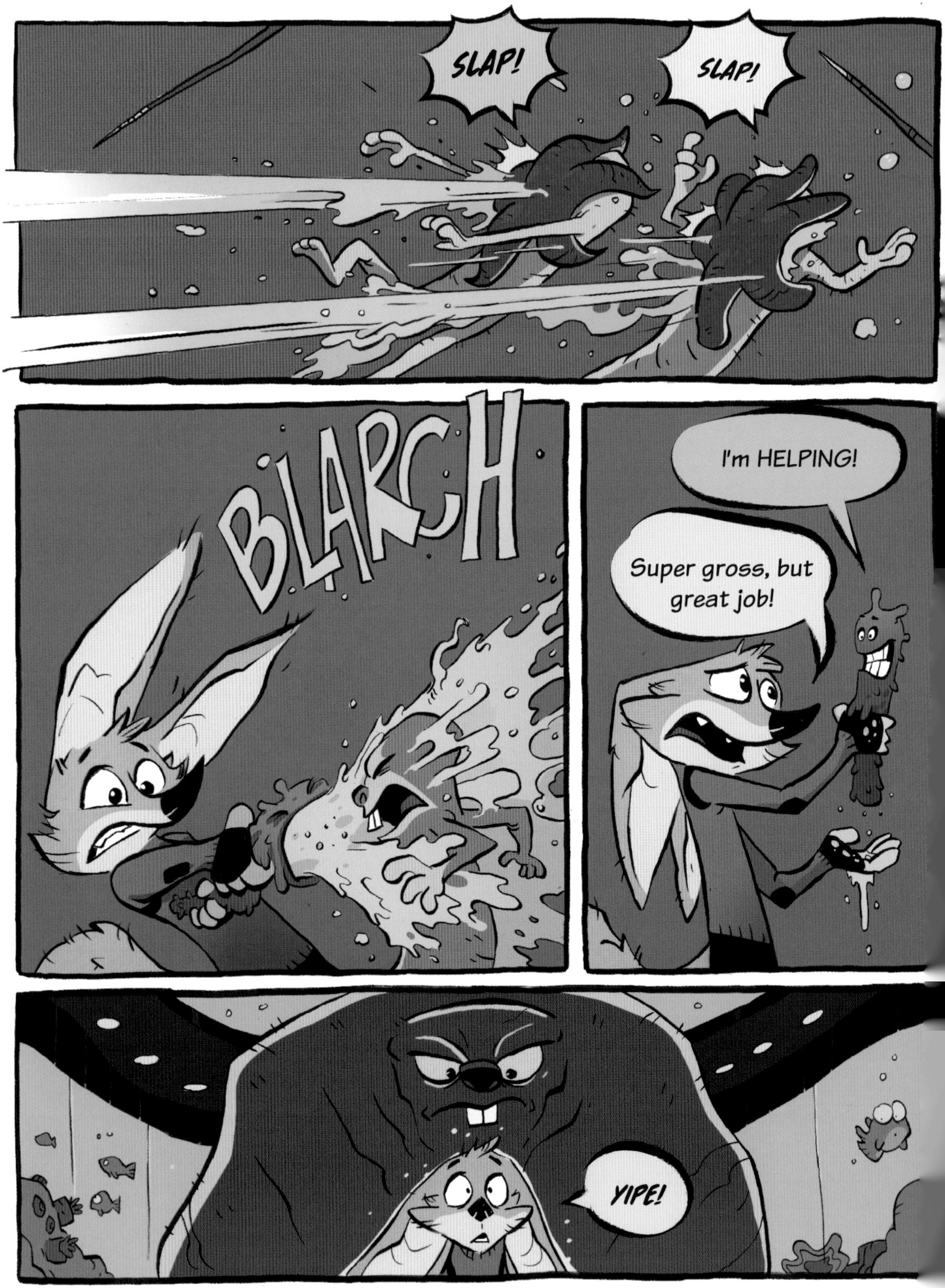
SLAP!
SLAP!
BLARCH
I'm HELPING!
Super gross, but great job!
YIPE!

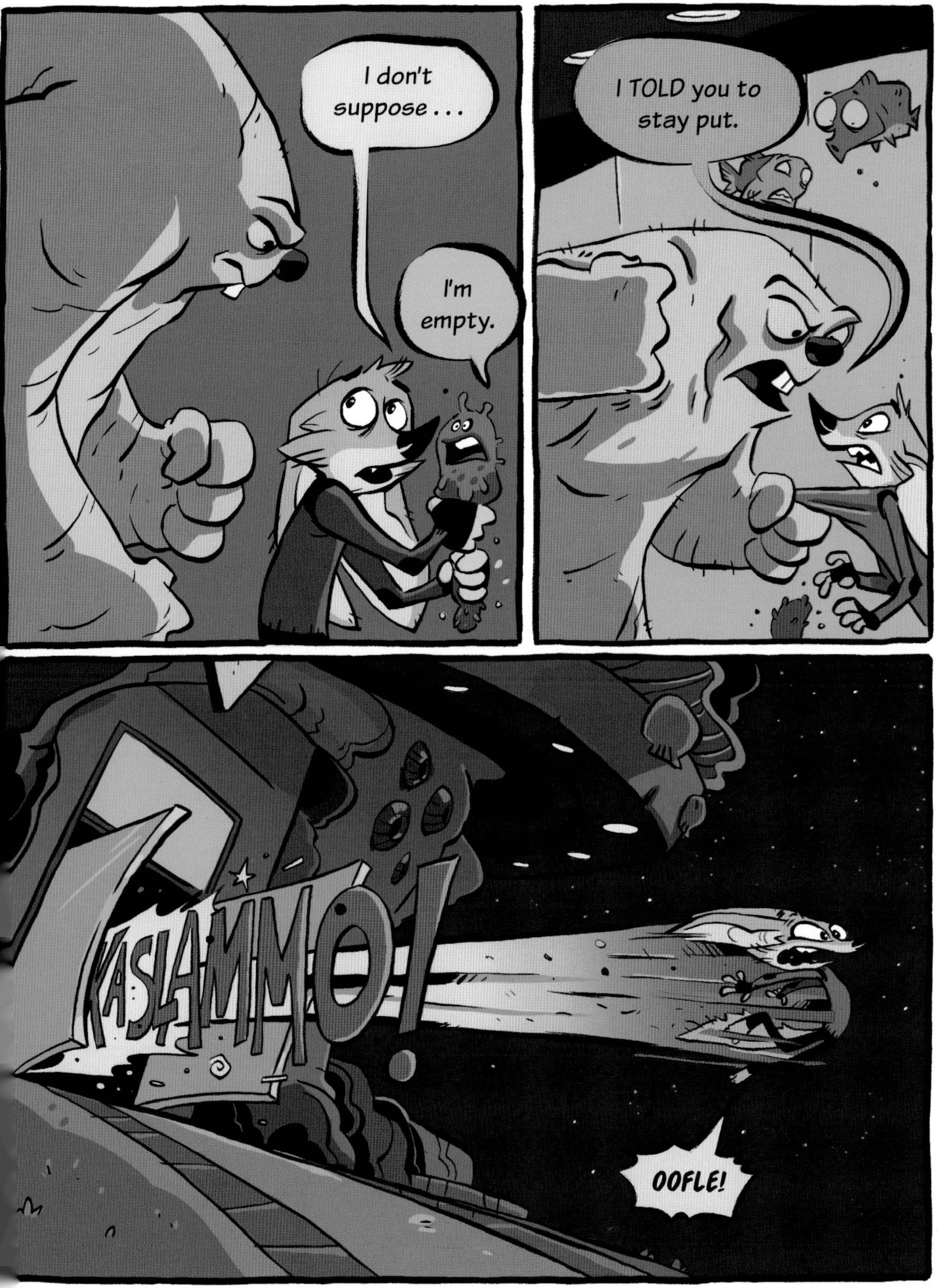
I don't suppose . . .
I'm empty.
I TOLD you to stay put.
KASLAMMO!
OOFLE!

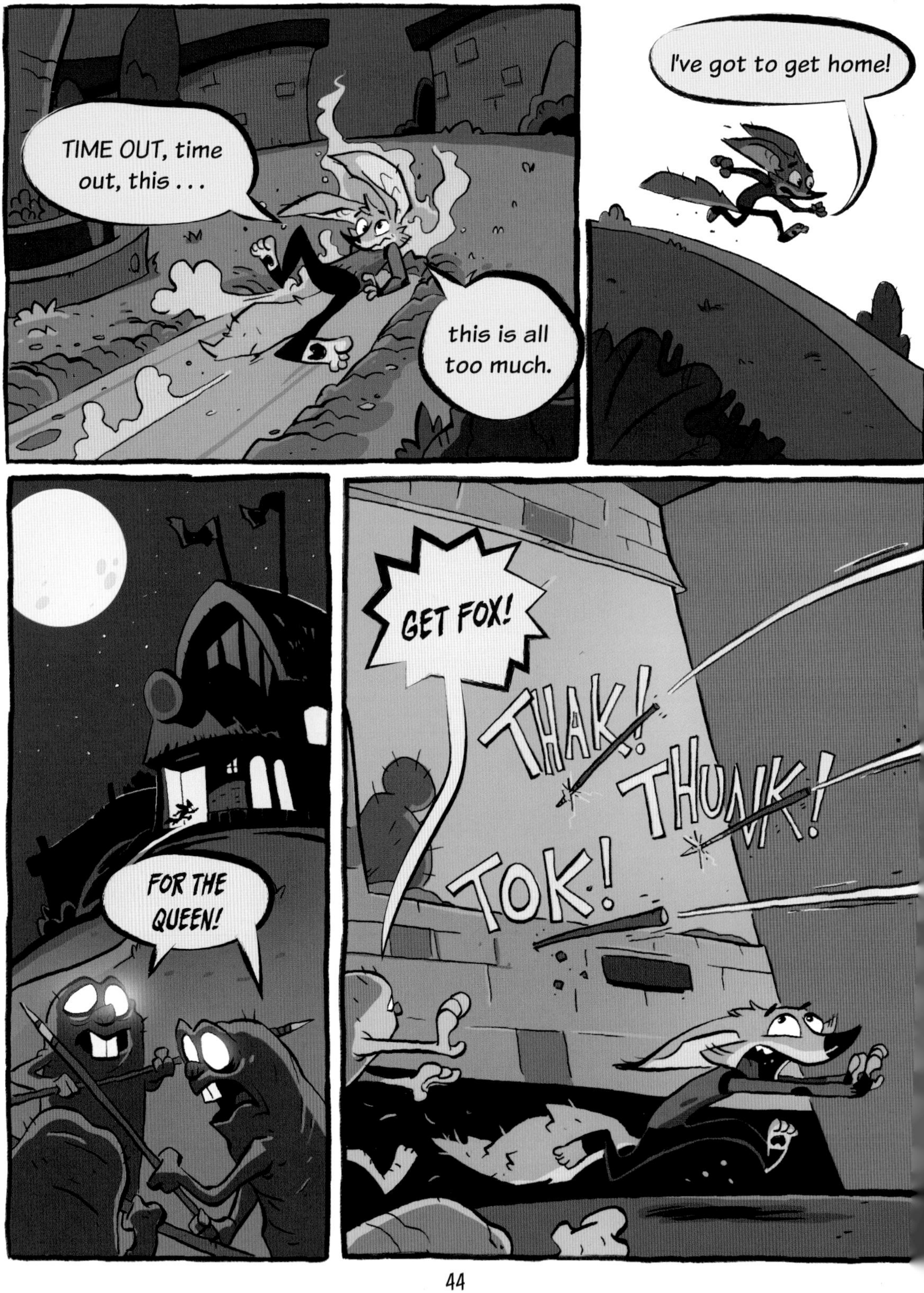
TIME OUT, time out, this . . .
this is all too much.
I've got to get home!
FOR THE QUEEN!
GET FOX!
THAK!
THUNK!
TOK!

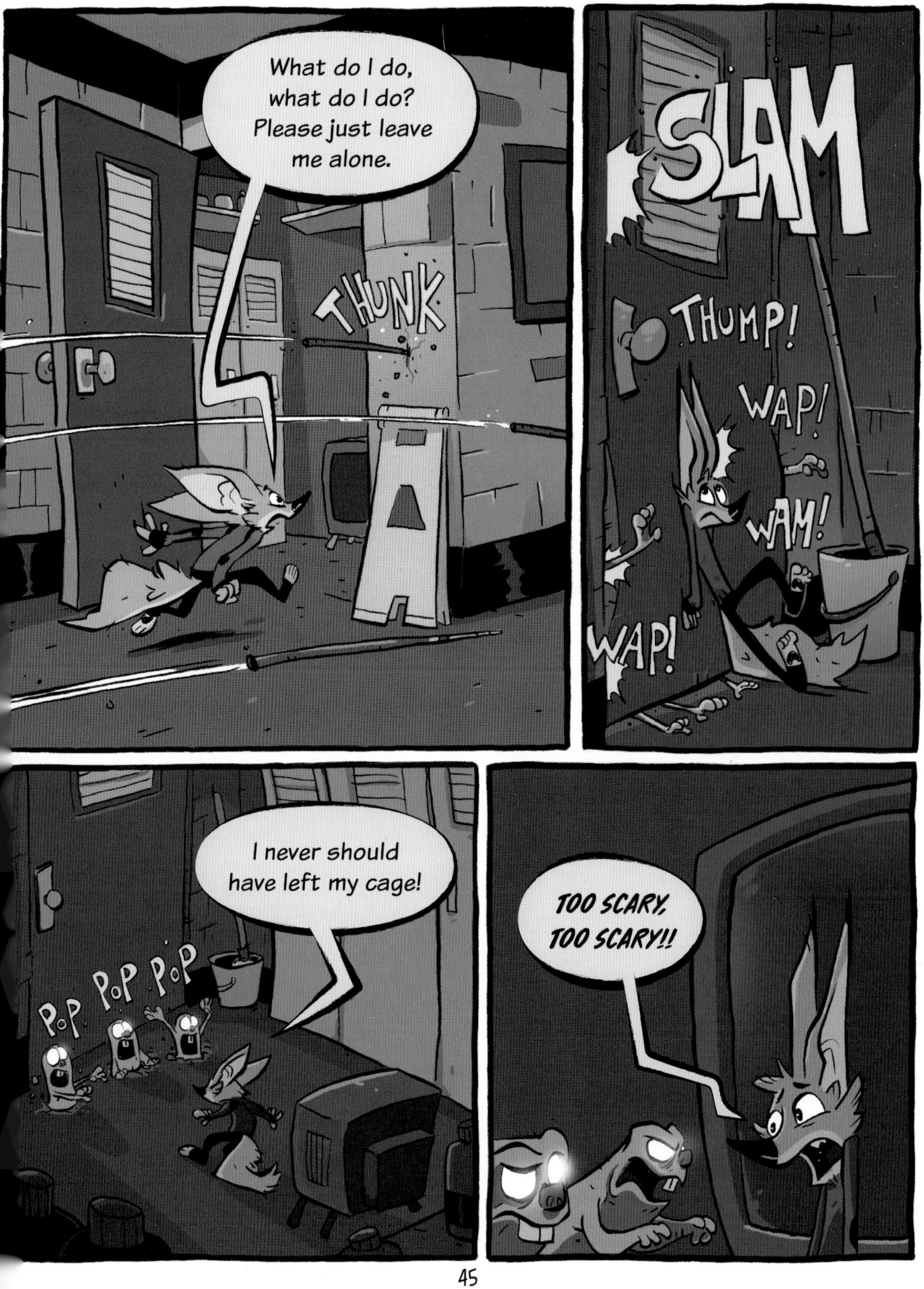
What do I do, what do I do? Please just leave me alone.
THUNK
SLAM
THUMP!
WAP!
WAM!
WAP!
I never should have left my cage!
PoP
PoP
PoP
PoP
TOO SCARY, TOO SCARY!!

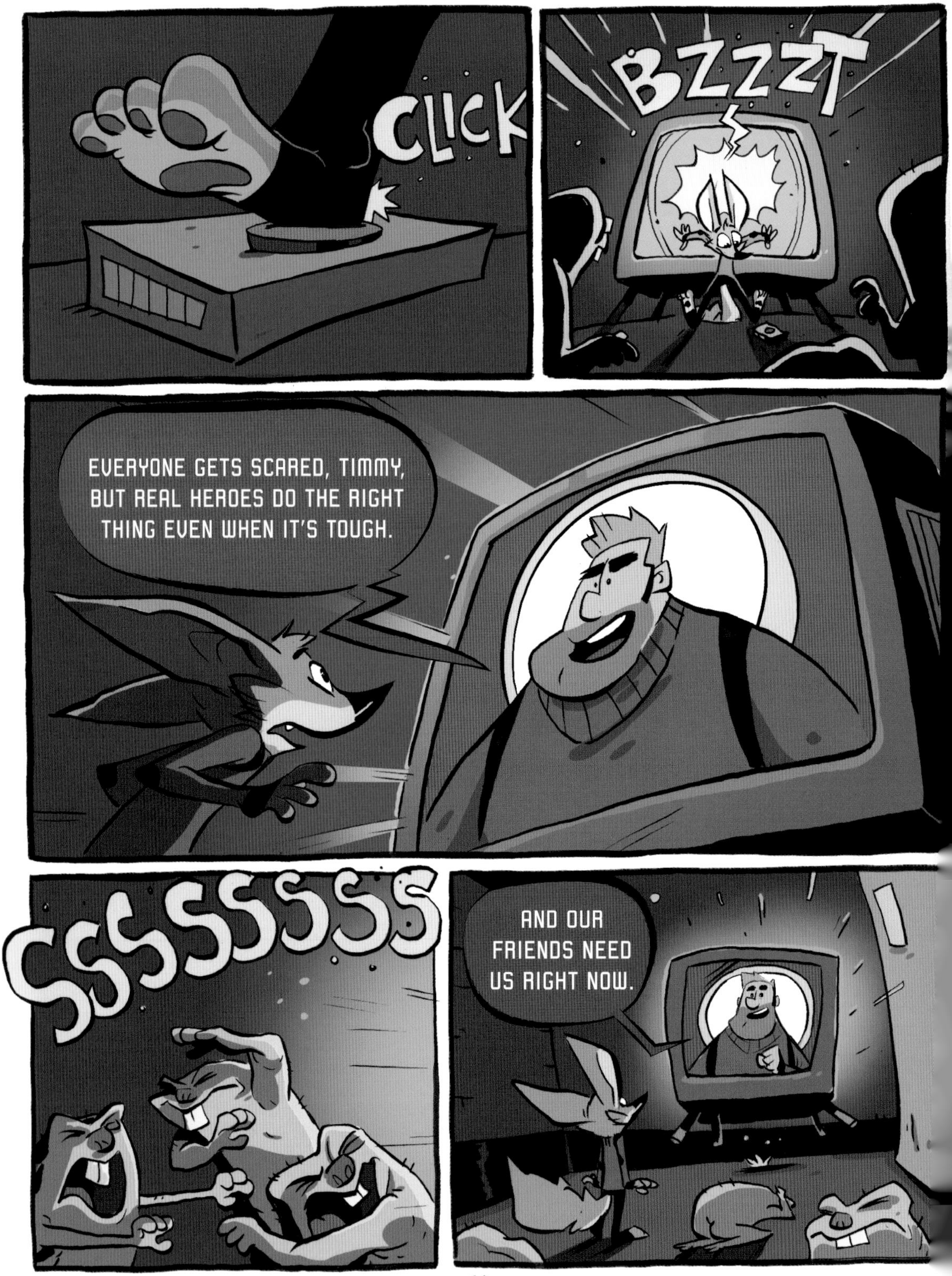
CLICK
BZZZT
EVERYONE GETS SCARED, TIMMY, BUT REAL HEROES DO THE RIGHT THING EVEN WHEN IT'S TOUGH.
SSSSSSSSS
AND OUR FRIENDS NEED US RIGHT NOW.

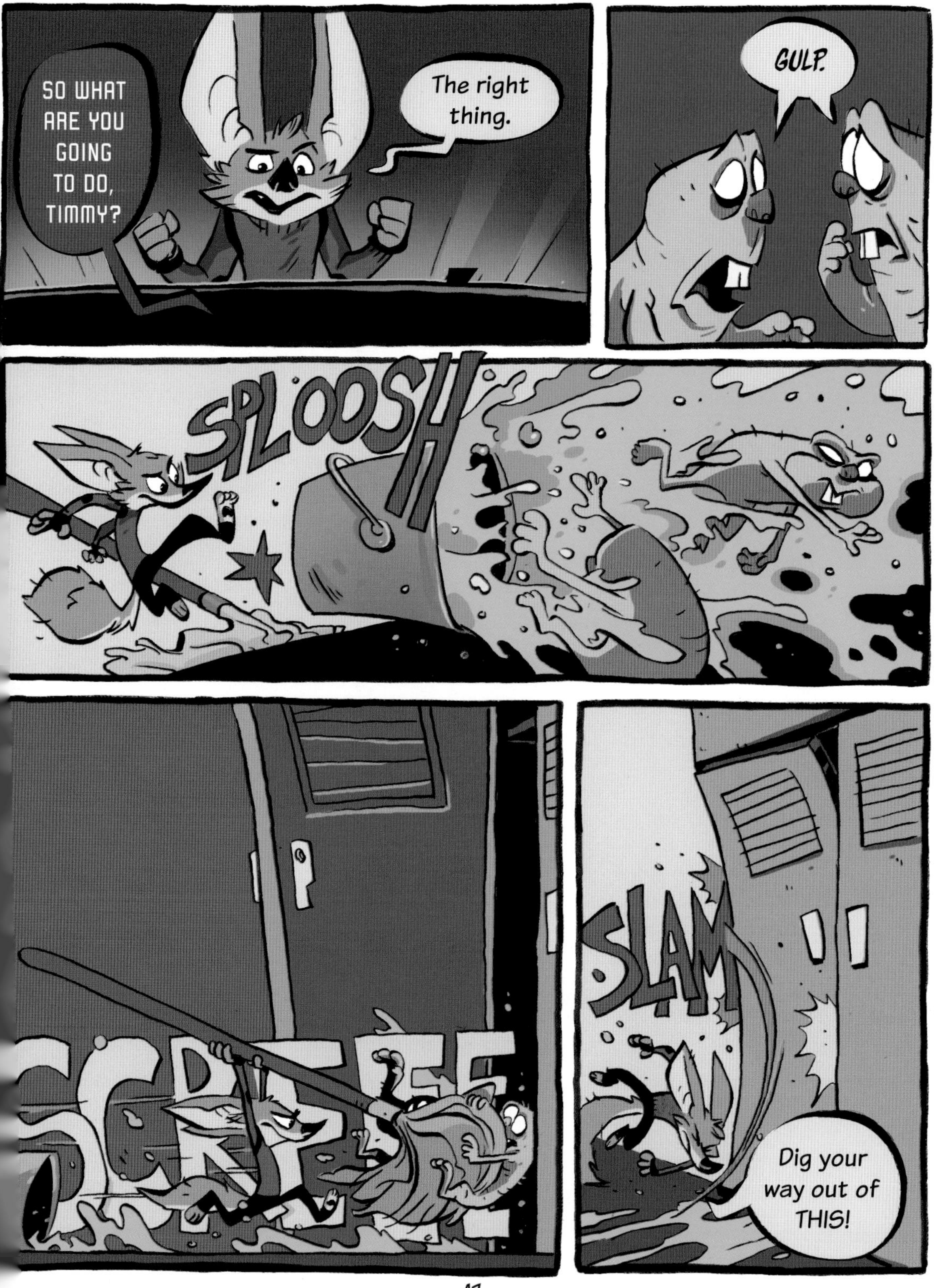
SO WHAT ARE YOU GOING TO DO, TIMMY?
The right thing.
GULP.
SPLOOSH
SLAM!!
Dig your way out of THIS!

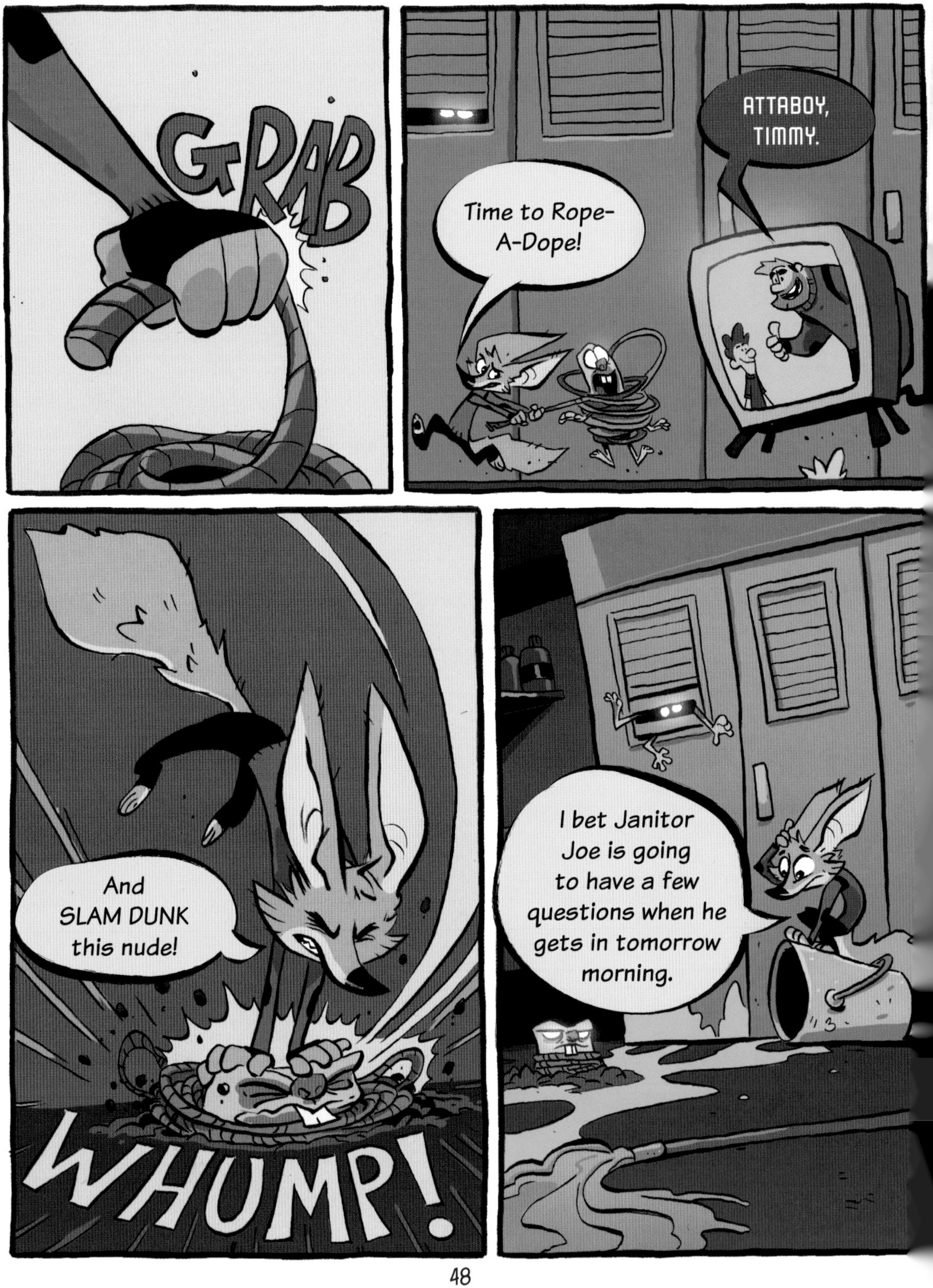
GRAB
Time to Rope-A-Dope!
ATTABOY, TIMMY.
And SLAM DUNK this nude!
WHUMP!
I bet Janitor Joe is going to have a few questions when he gets in tomorrow morning.

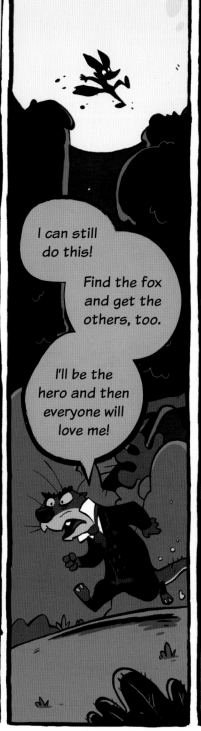

Now I just have to reach the bug house and avoid an angry mob and spear-flinging mole rats!

I can still do this!

Find the fox and get the others, too.

I'll be the hero and then everyone will love me!

At least we got my tire swing back.

Forget that, what's up with all these toothpicks everywhere?

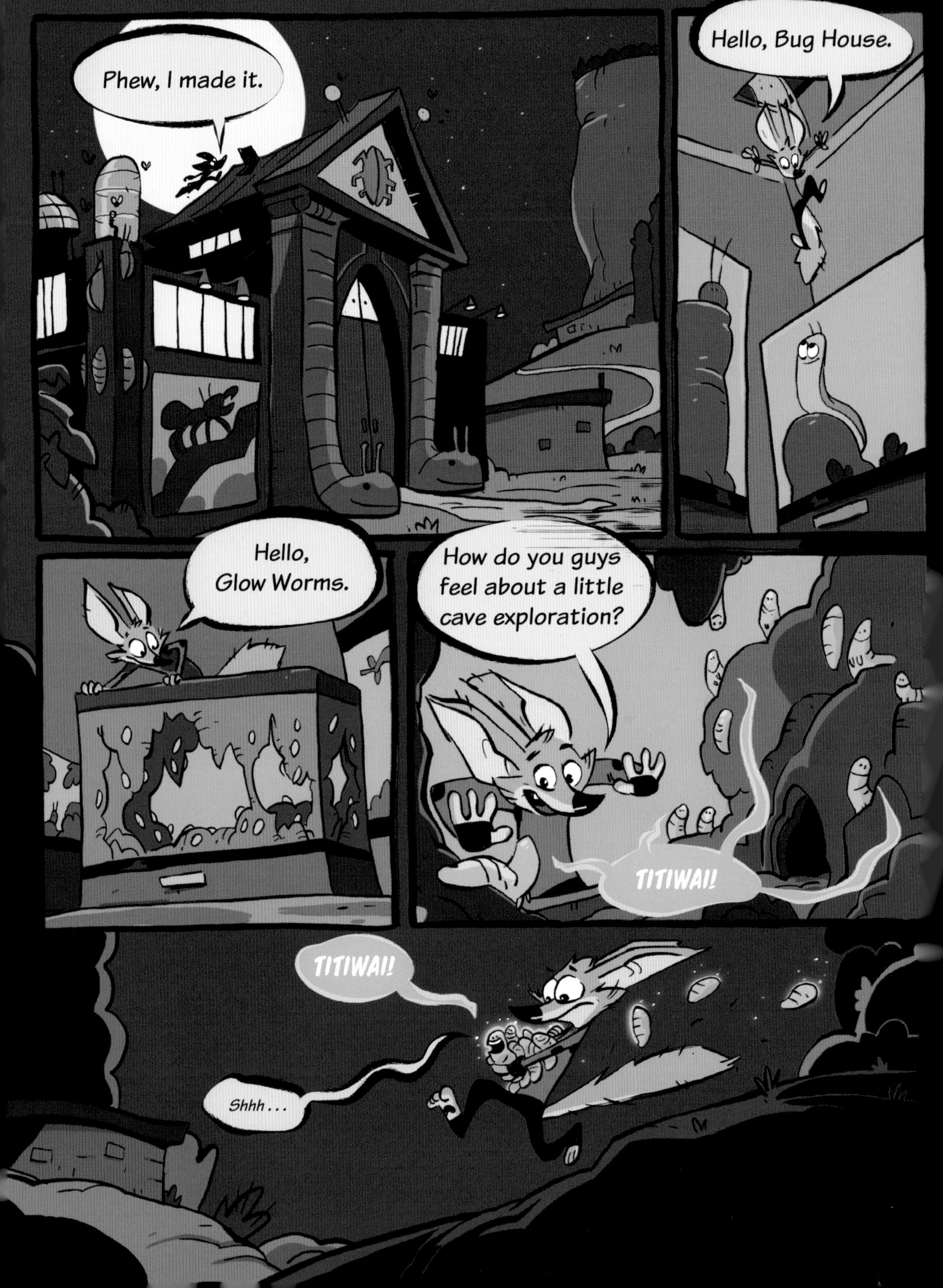
Phew, I made it.
Hello, Bug House.
Hello, Glow Worms.
How do you guys feel about a little cave exploration?
TITIWAI!
TITIWAI!
Shhh . . .

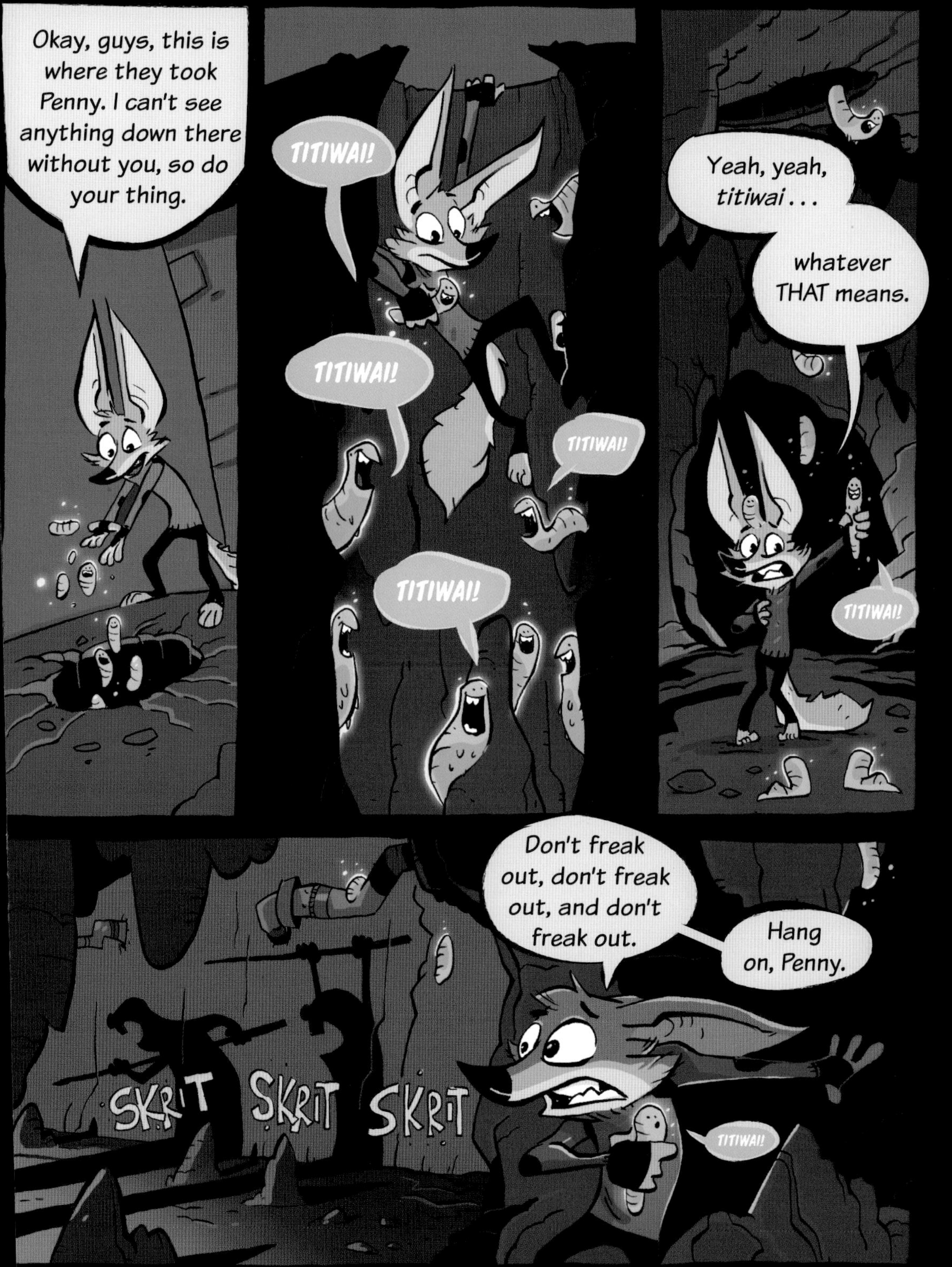
Okay, guys, this is where they took Penny. I can't see anything down there without you, so do your thing.
TITIWAI!
TITIWAI!
TITIWAI!
TITIWAI!
Yeah, yeah, *titiwai*...
whatever THAT means.
TITIWAI!
SKRIT SKRIT SKRIT
Don't freak out, don't freak out, and don't freak out.
Hang on, Penny.
TITIWAI!

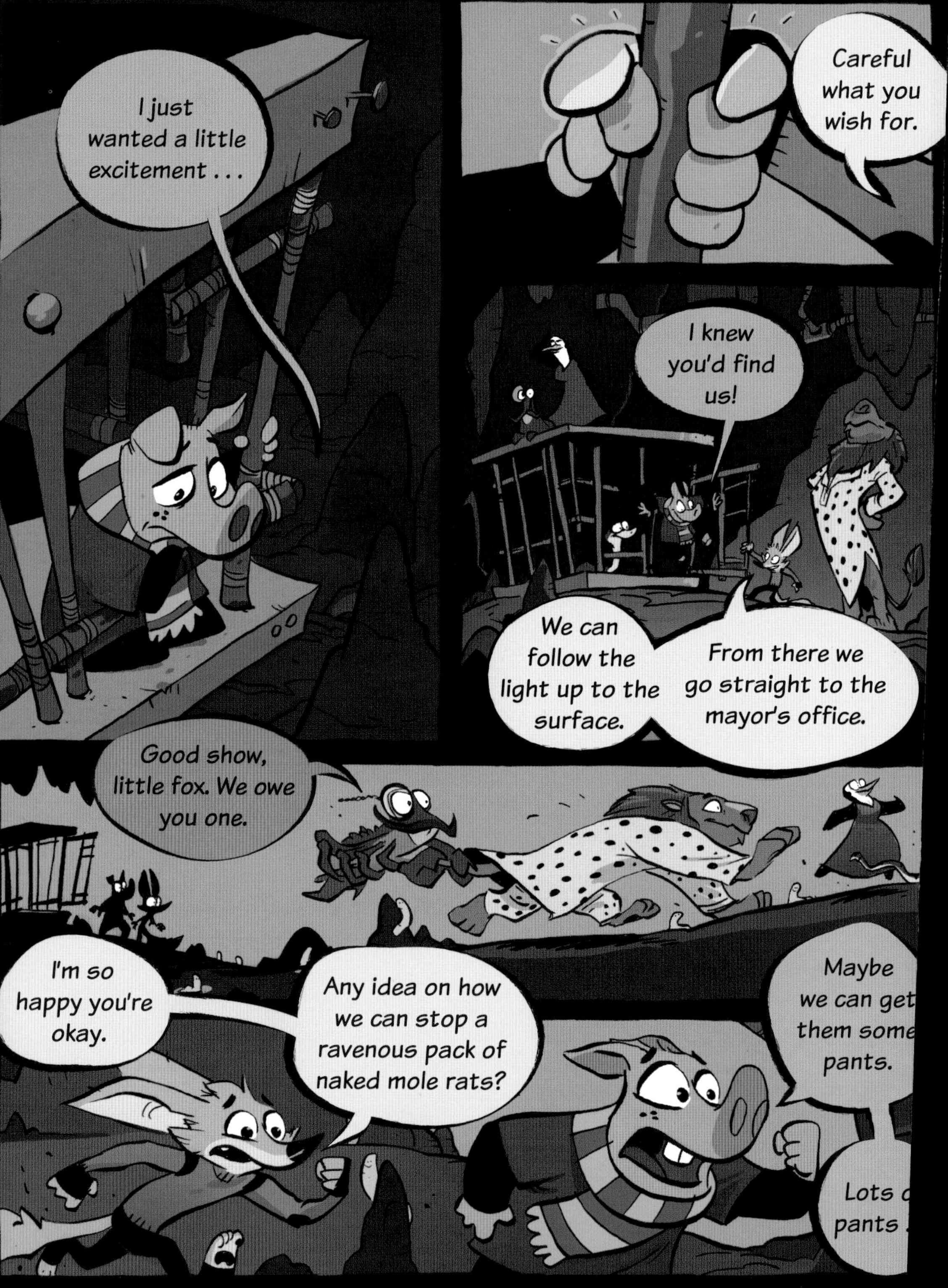
I just wanted a little excitement . . .
Careful what you wish for.
I knew you'd find us!
We can follow the light up to the surface.
From there we go straight to the mayor's office.
Good show, little fox. We owe you one.
I'm so happy you're okay.
Any idea on how we can stop a ravenous pack of naked mole rats?
Maybe we can get them some pants.
Lots of pants . . .

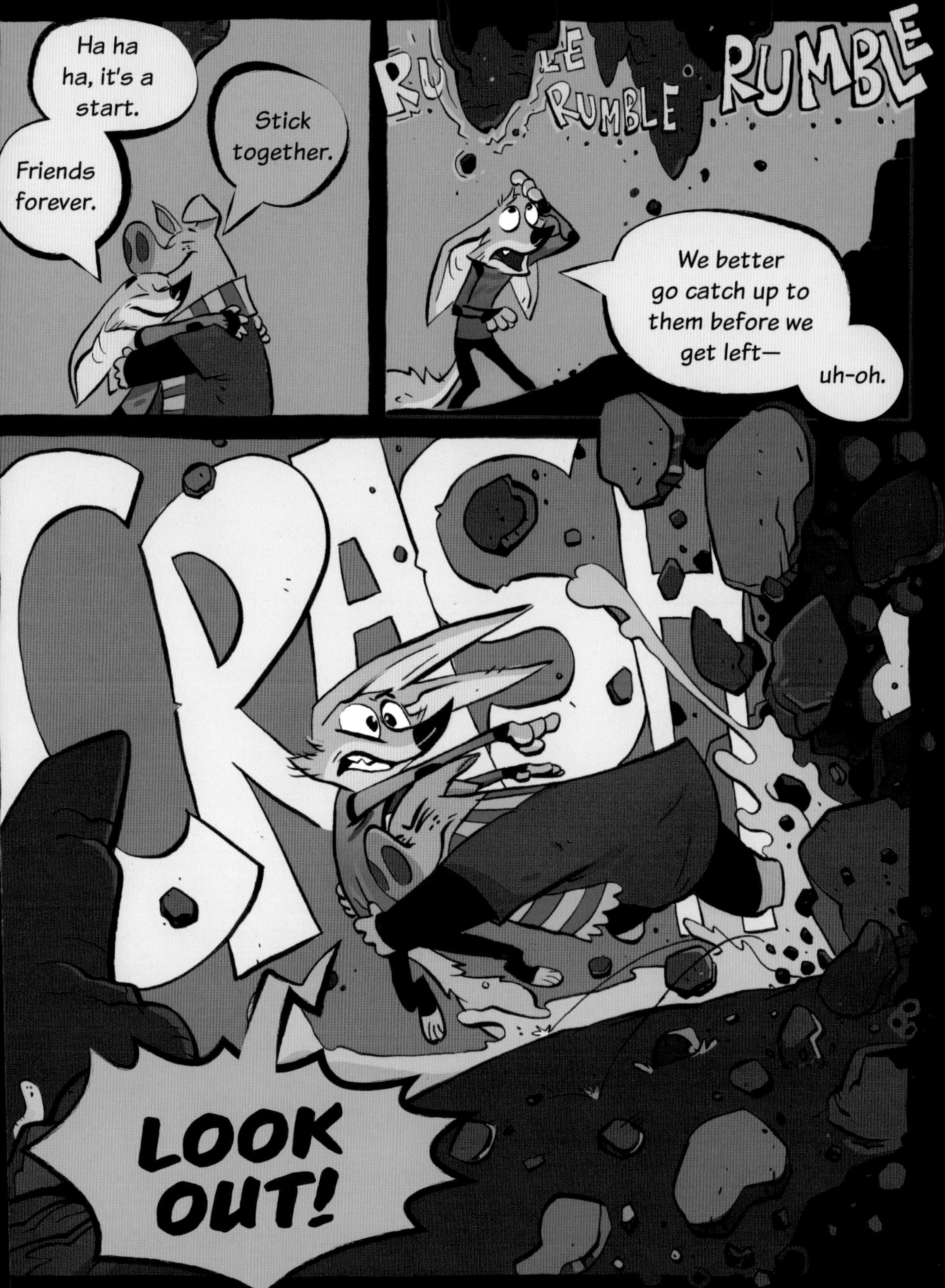
Ha ha ha, it's a start.
Friends forever.
Stick together.
RUMBLE RUMBLE RUMBLE
We better go catch up to them before we get left—
uh-oh.
CRASH
LOOK OUT!

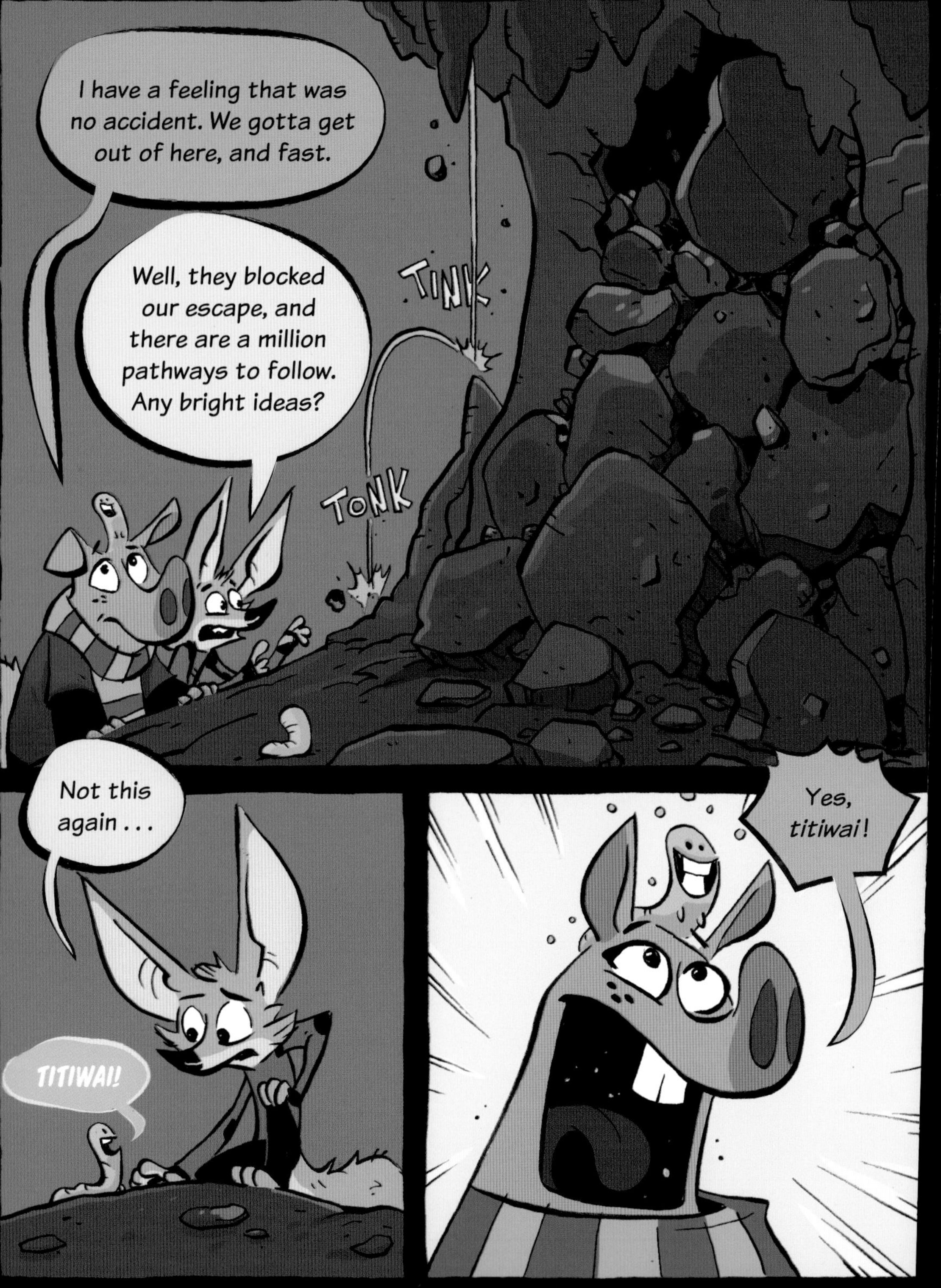
I have a feeling that was no accident. We gotta get out of here, and fast.
Well, they blocked our escape, and there are a million pathways to follow. Any bright ideas?
TINK
TONK
Not this again . . .
TITIWAI!
Yes, titiwai!

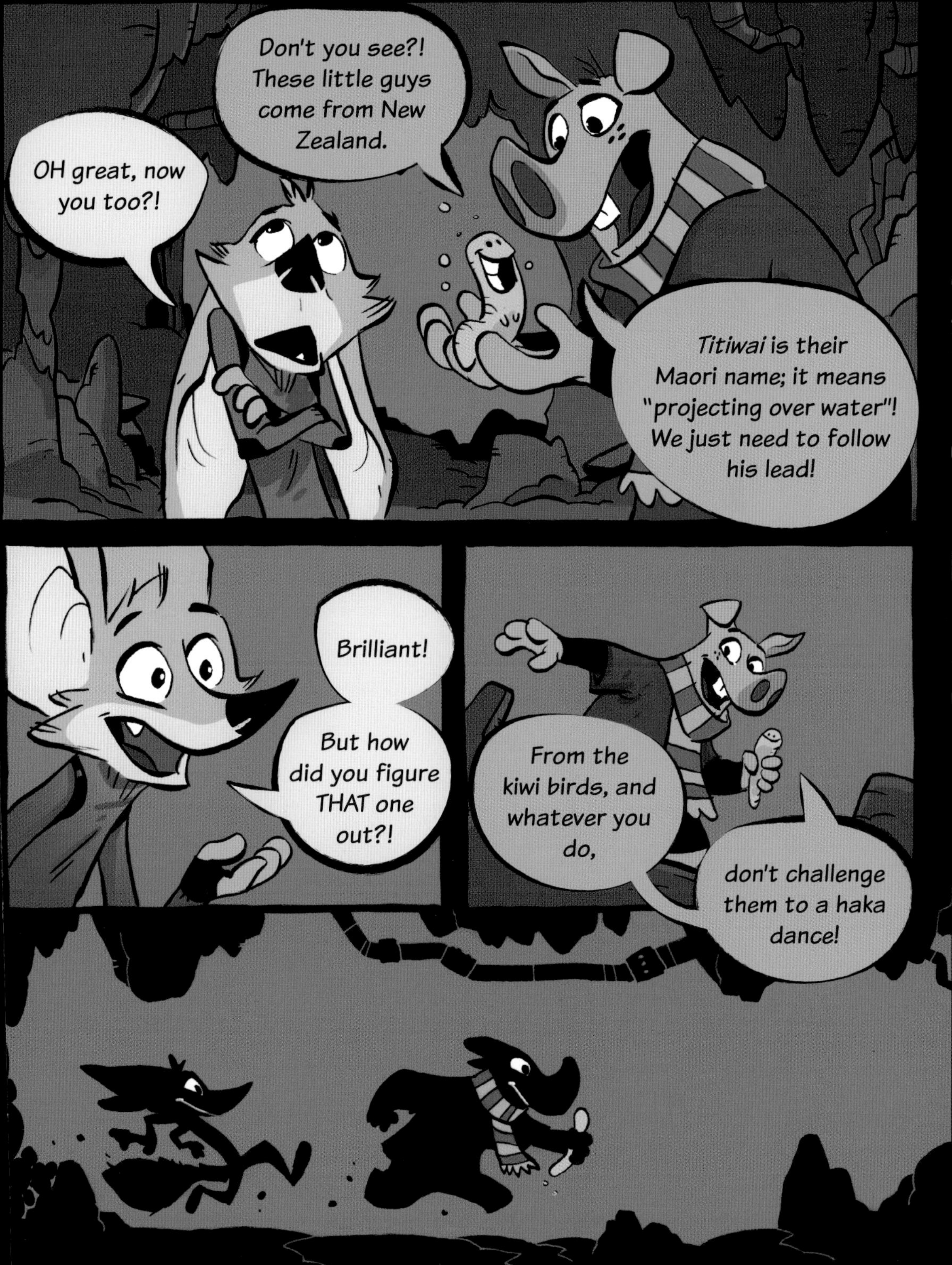

Don't you see?! These little guys come from New Zealand.
OH great, now you too?!
Titiwai is their Maori name; it means "projecting over water"! We just need to follow his lead!
Brilliant!
But how did you figure THAT one out?!
From the kiwi birds, and whatever you do,
don't challenge them to a haka dance!

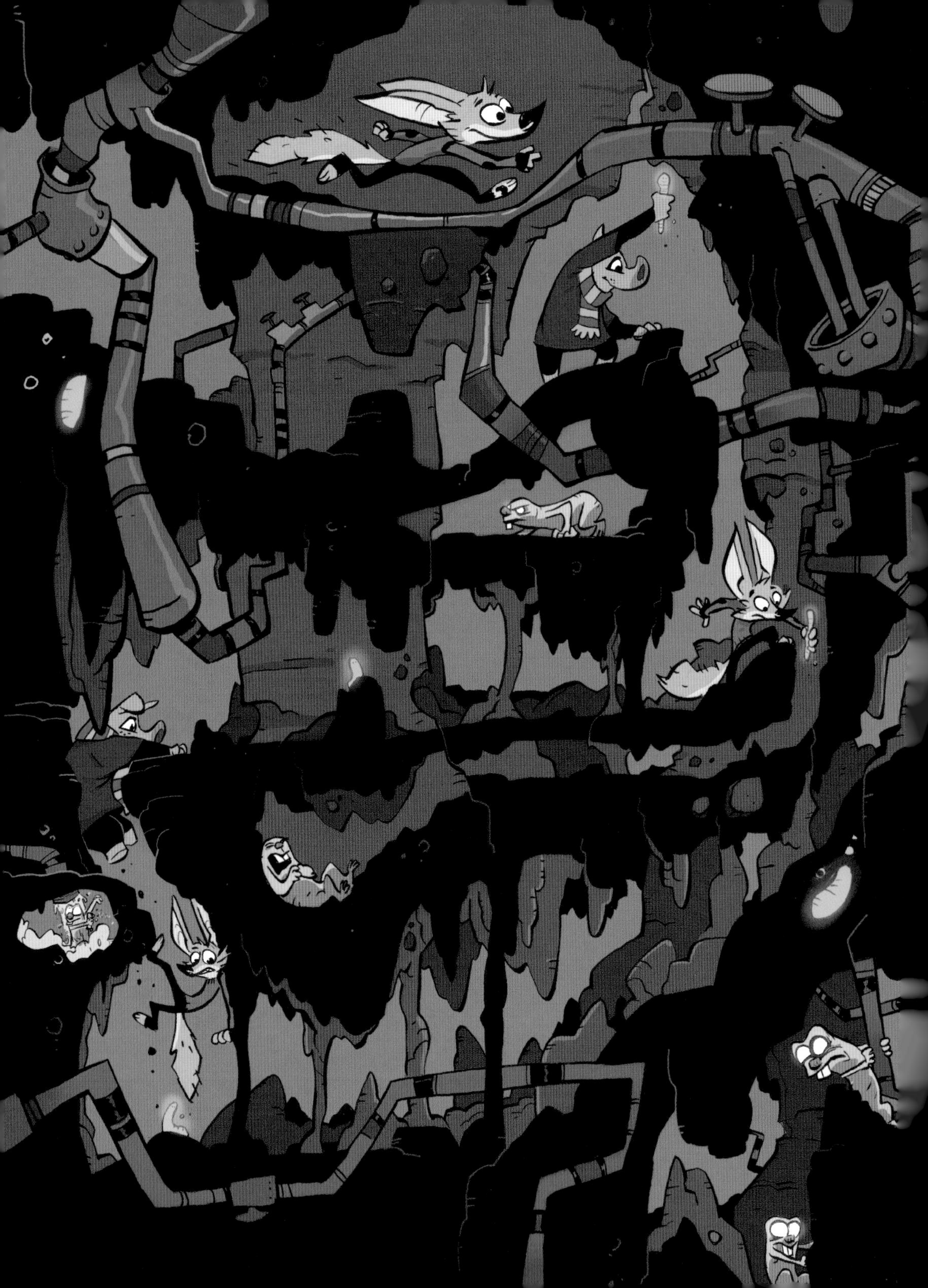

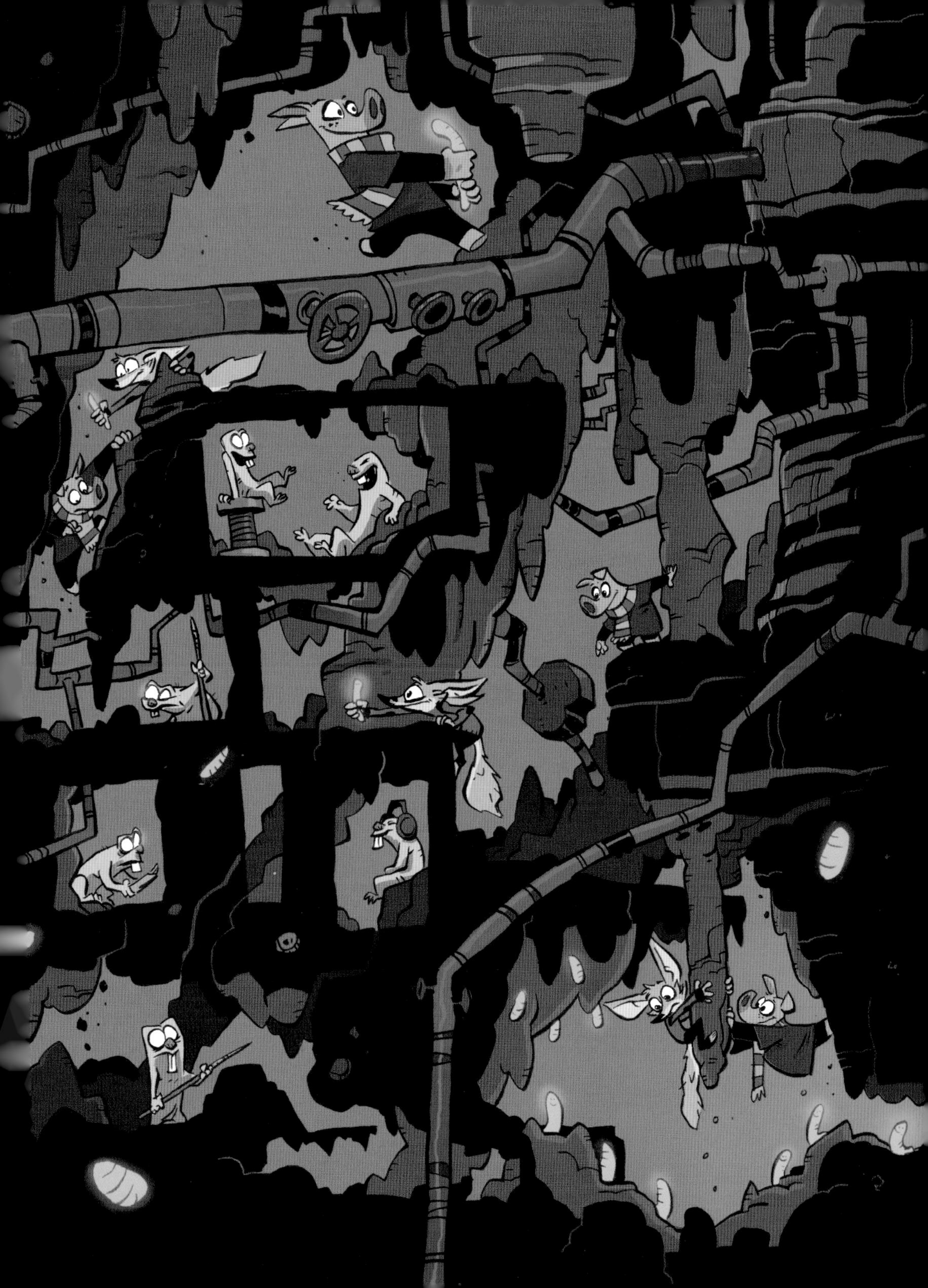

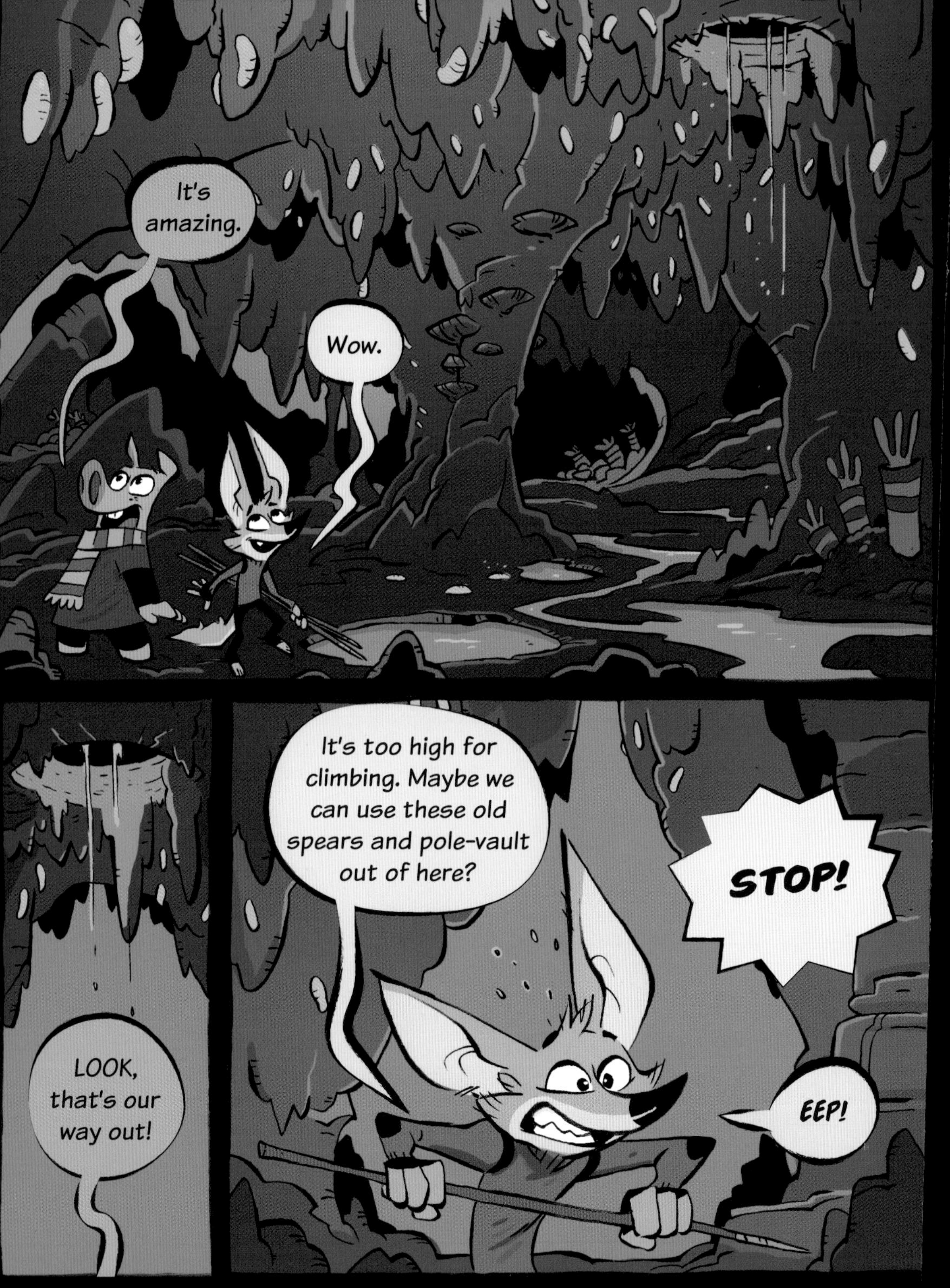
It's amazing.
Wow.
LOOK, that's our way out!
It's too high for climbing. Maybe we can use these old spears and pole-vault out of here?
STOP!
EEP!

Well, I hope you're happy.
You've ruined everything, and this animal kingdom will suffer for it.
I had such big dreams for Wild Zoo Yonder.
We would buy locally and recycle everything!
Landscape immersion using only rocks and plants from where the animals naturally come from, making them feel more at home!
We'd recycle every last bit of poop just to fertilize a lawn for concerts in the park.
I even had the Beetles lined up to play . . . Do you know how hard it was to get them?!?!
It would have looked so nice. The animals would have been so happy, but you've ruined all of that by trying to stop me.

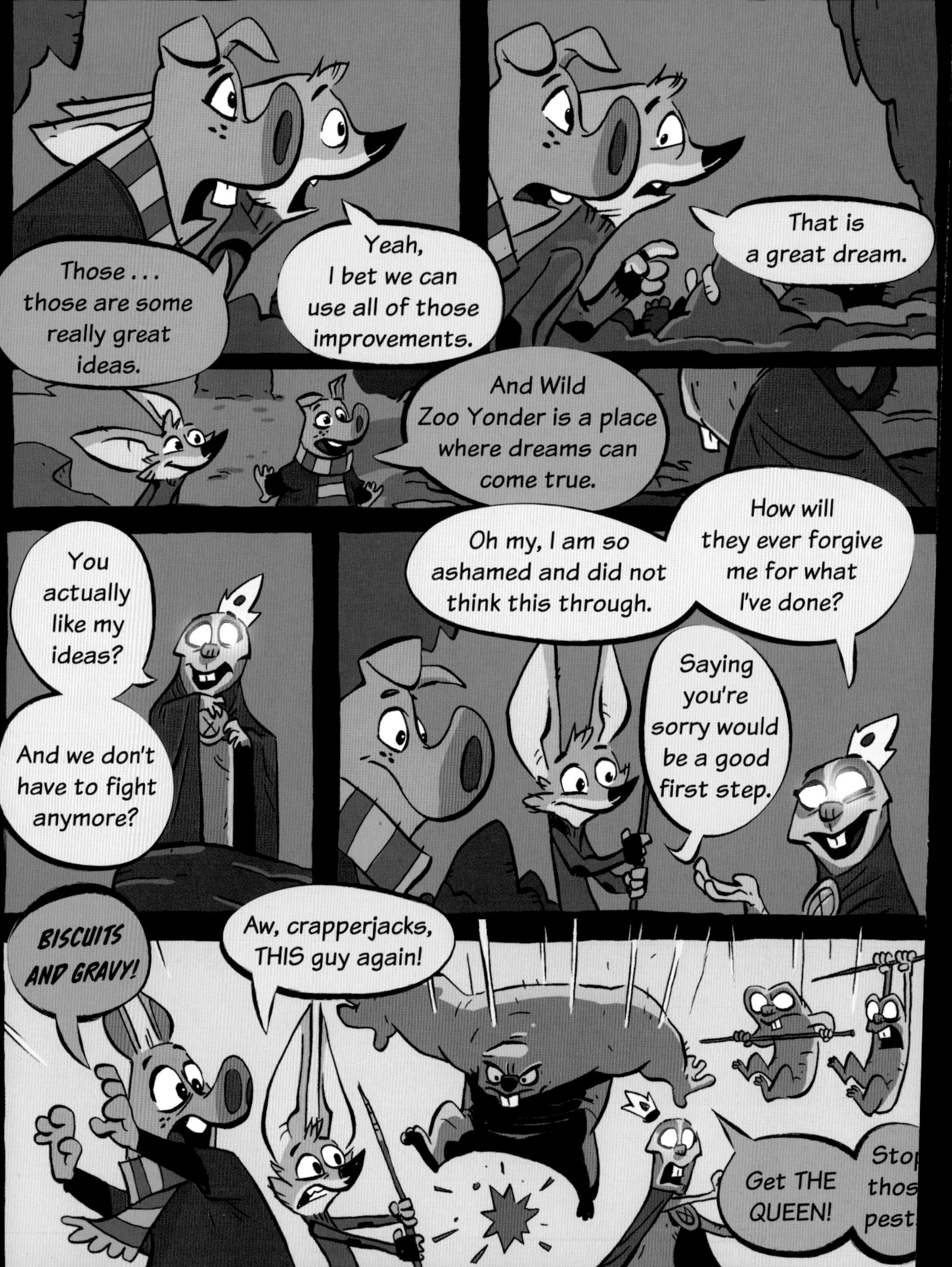
Those . . . those are some really great ideas.
Yeah, I bet we can use all of those improvements.
That is a great dream.
And Wild Zoo Yonder is a place where dreams can come true.
You actually like my ideas?
And we don't have to fight anymore?
Oh my, I am so ashamed and did not think this through.
How will they ever forgive me for what I've done?
Saying you're sorry would be a good first step.
BISCUITS AND GRAVY!
Aw, crapperjacks, THIS guy again!
Get THE QUEEN!

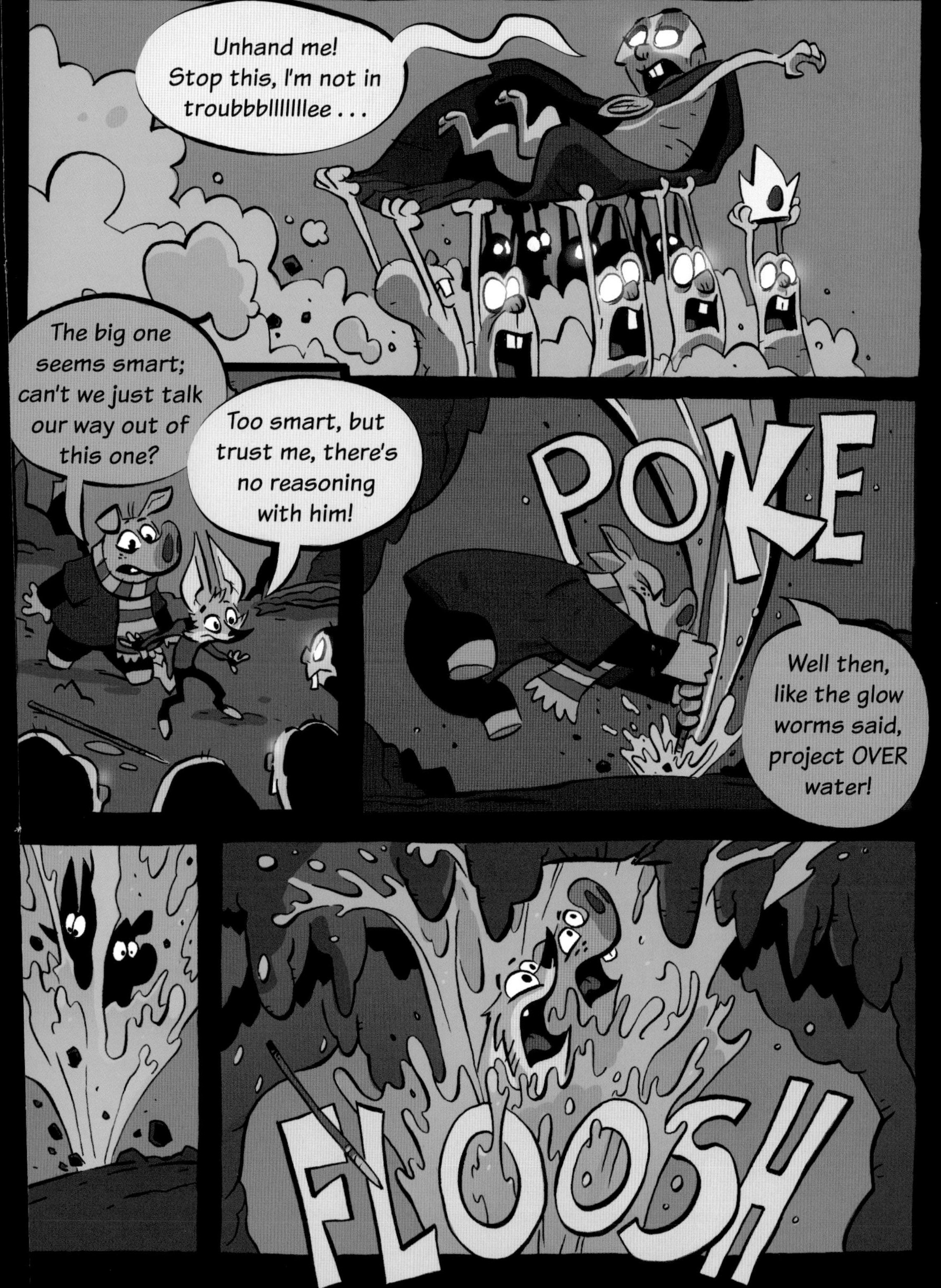
Unhand me! Stop this, I'm not in troubbbllllllee . . .
The big one seems smart; can't we just talk our way out of this one?
Too smart, but trust me, there's no reasoning with him!
POKE
Well then, like the glow worms said, project OVER water!
FLOOSH

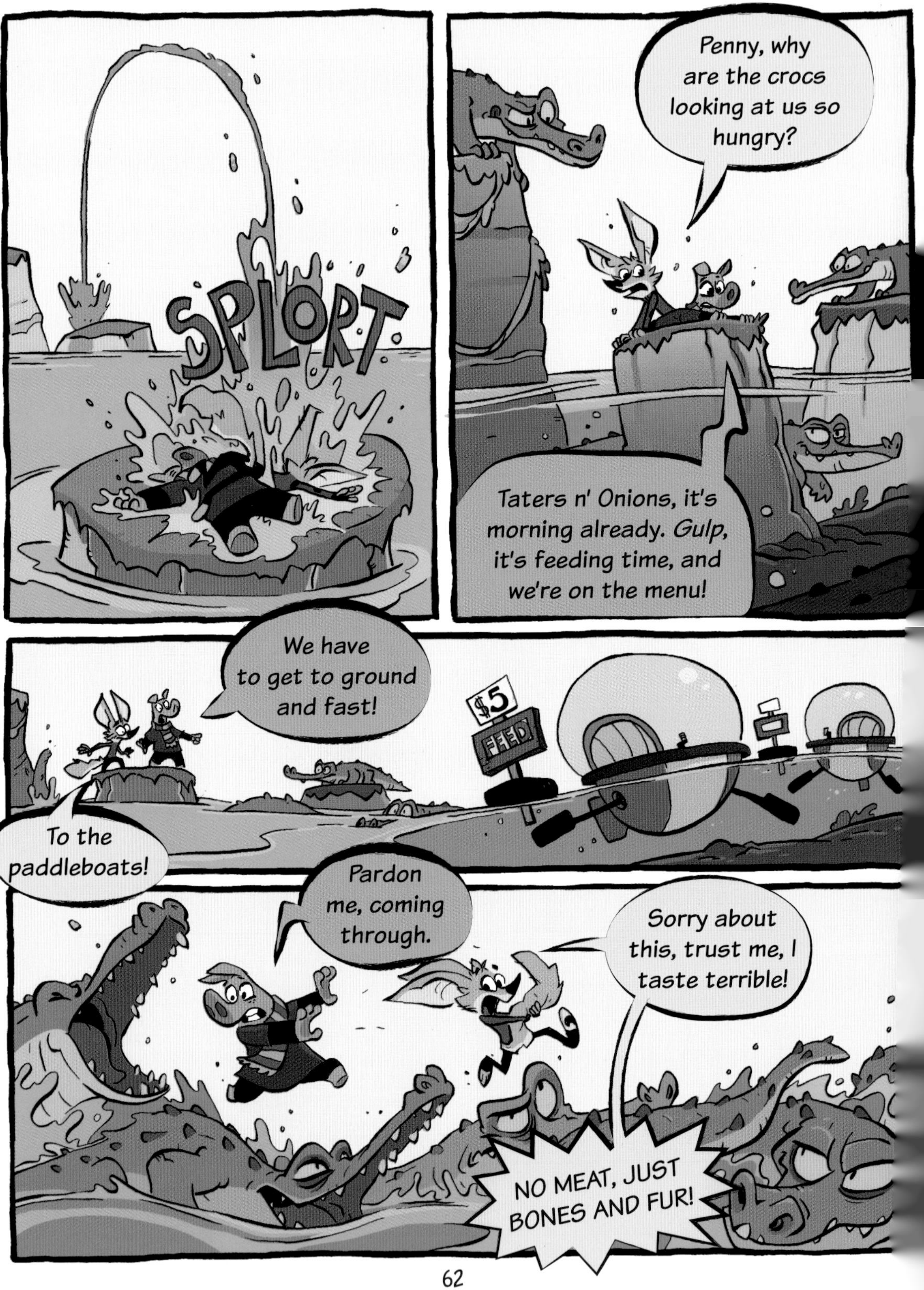
SPLORT
Penny, why are the crocs looking at us so hungry?
Taters n' Onions, it's morning already. *Gulp*, it's feeding time, and we're on the menu!
We have to get to ground and fast!
$5
FEED
To the paddleboats!
Pardon me, coming through.
Sorry about this, trust me, I taste terrible!
NO MEAT, JUST BONES AND FUR!

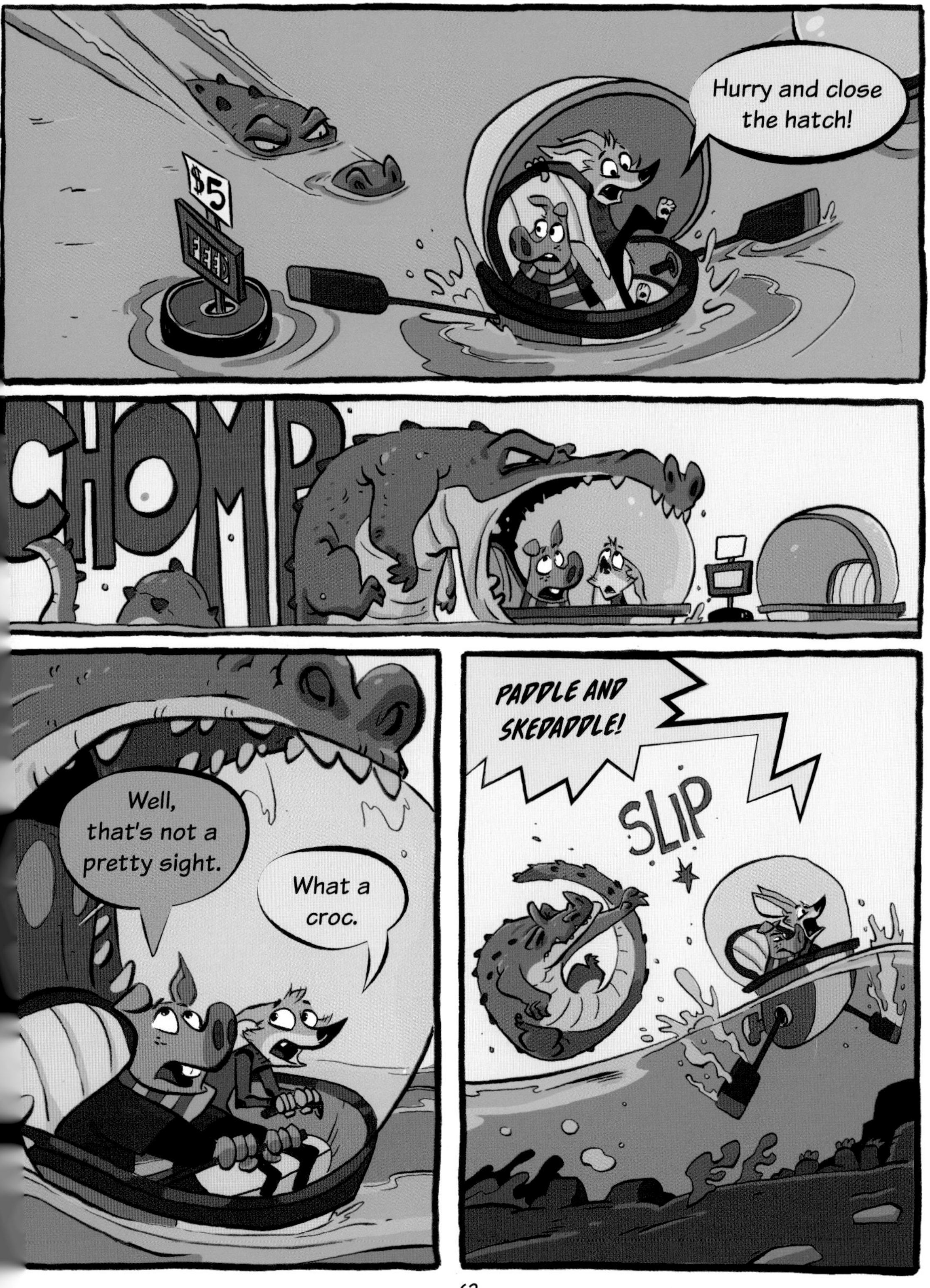
Hurry and close the hatch!
$5
FEED
CHOMP
Well, that's not a pretty sight.
What a croc.
PADDLE AND SKEDADDLE!
SLIP

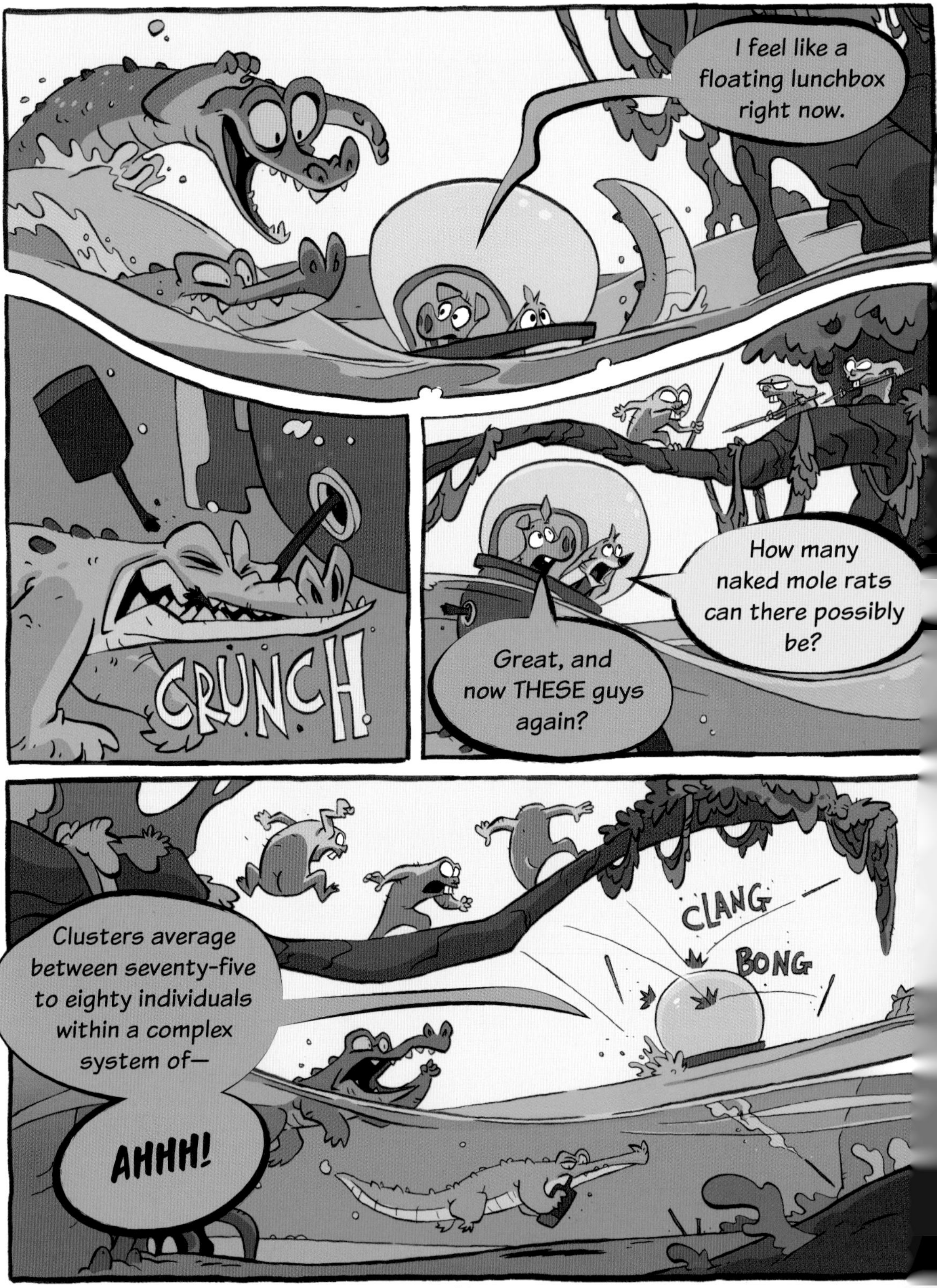
I feel like a floating lunchbox right now.
CRUNCH
How many naked mole rats can there possibly be?
Great, and now THESE guys again?
Clusters average between seventy-five to eighty individuals within a complex system of—
AHHH!
CLANG
BONG

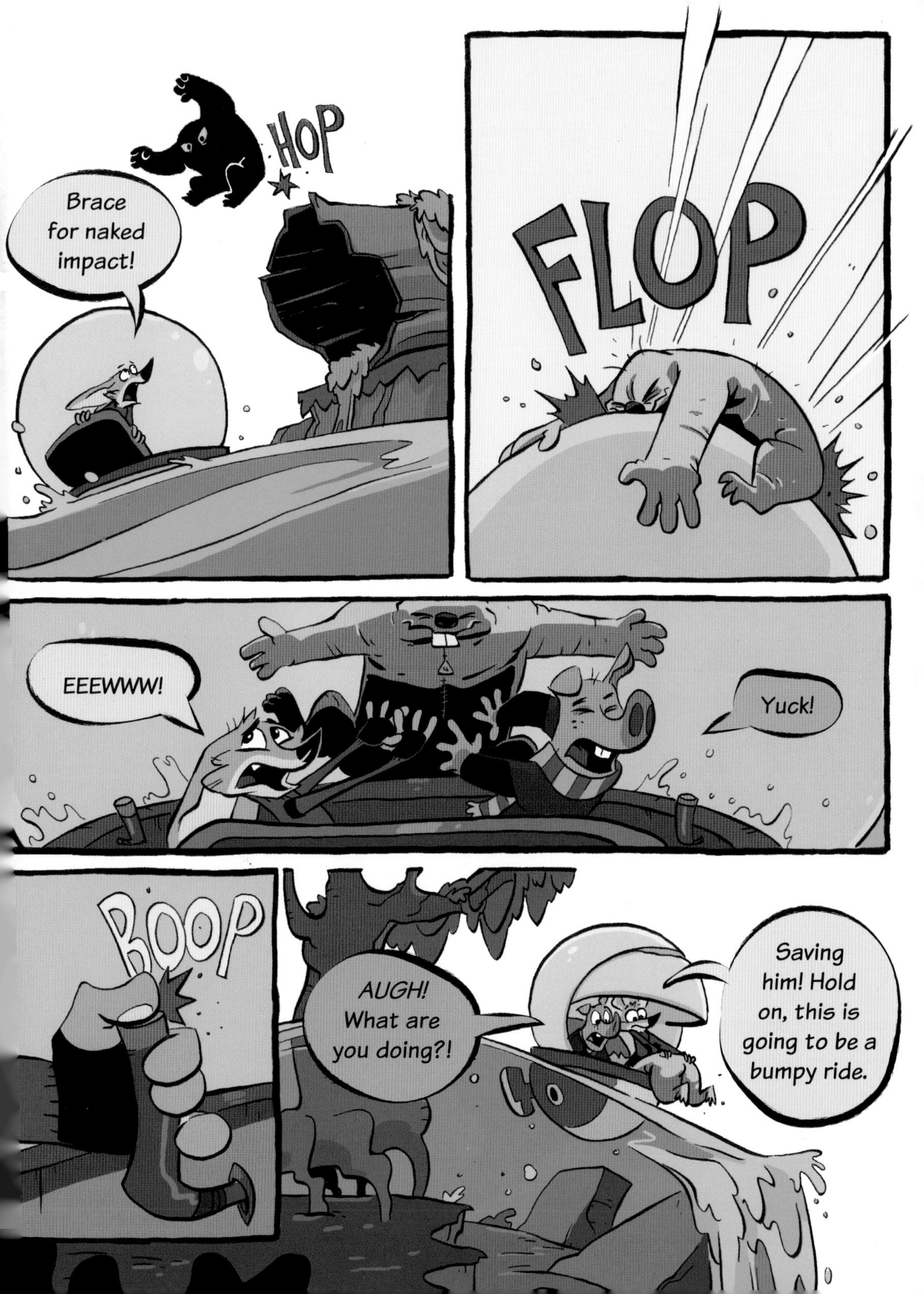
HOP
Brace for naked impact!
FLOP
EEEWWW!
Yuck!
BOOP
AUGH! What are you doing?!
Saving him! Hold on, this is going to be a bumpy ride.

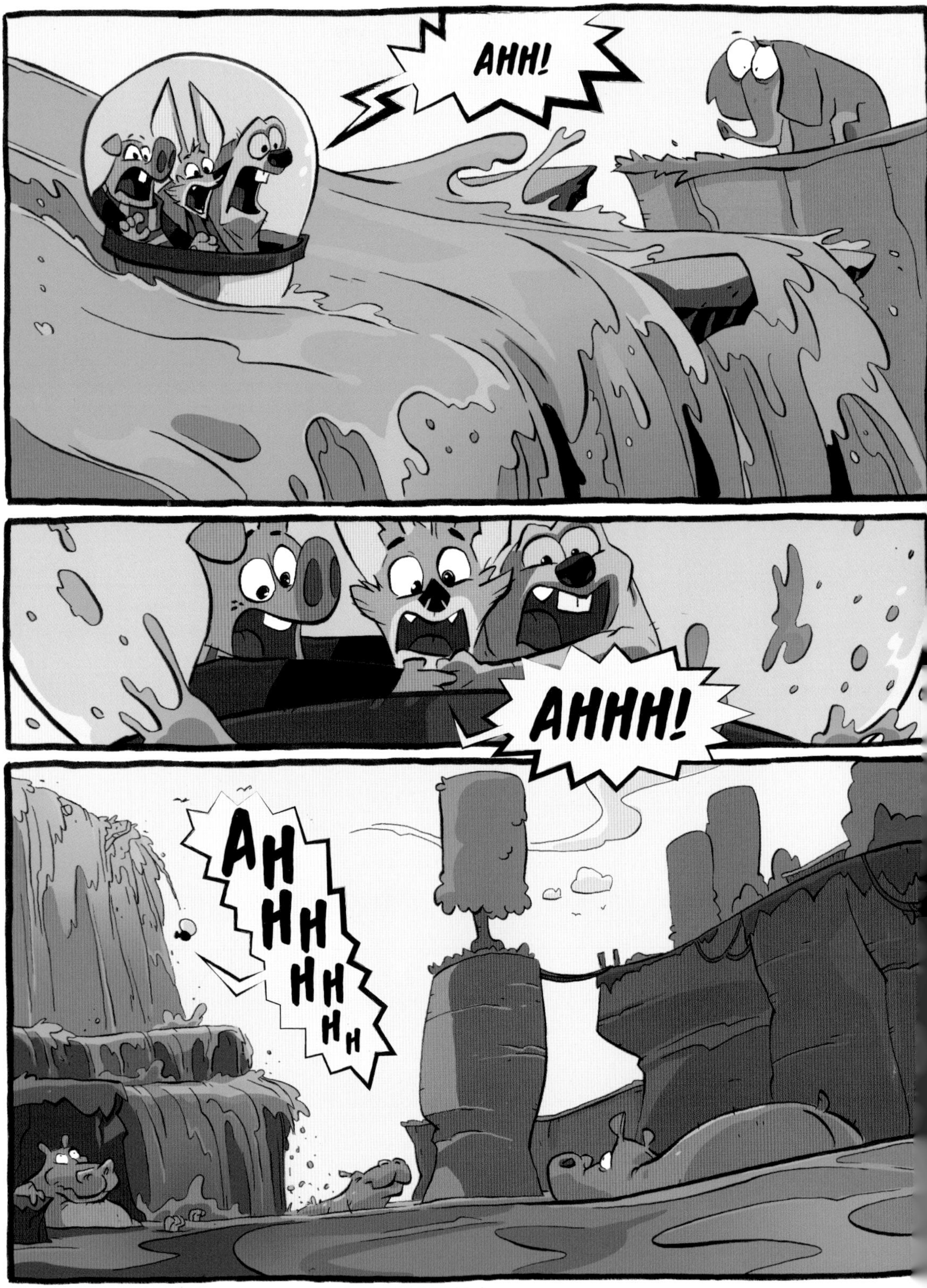
AHH!
AHHH!
AHHHHHHHH

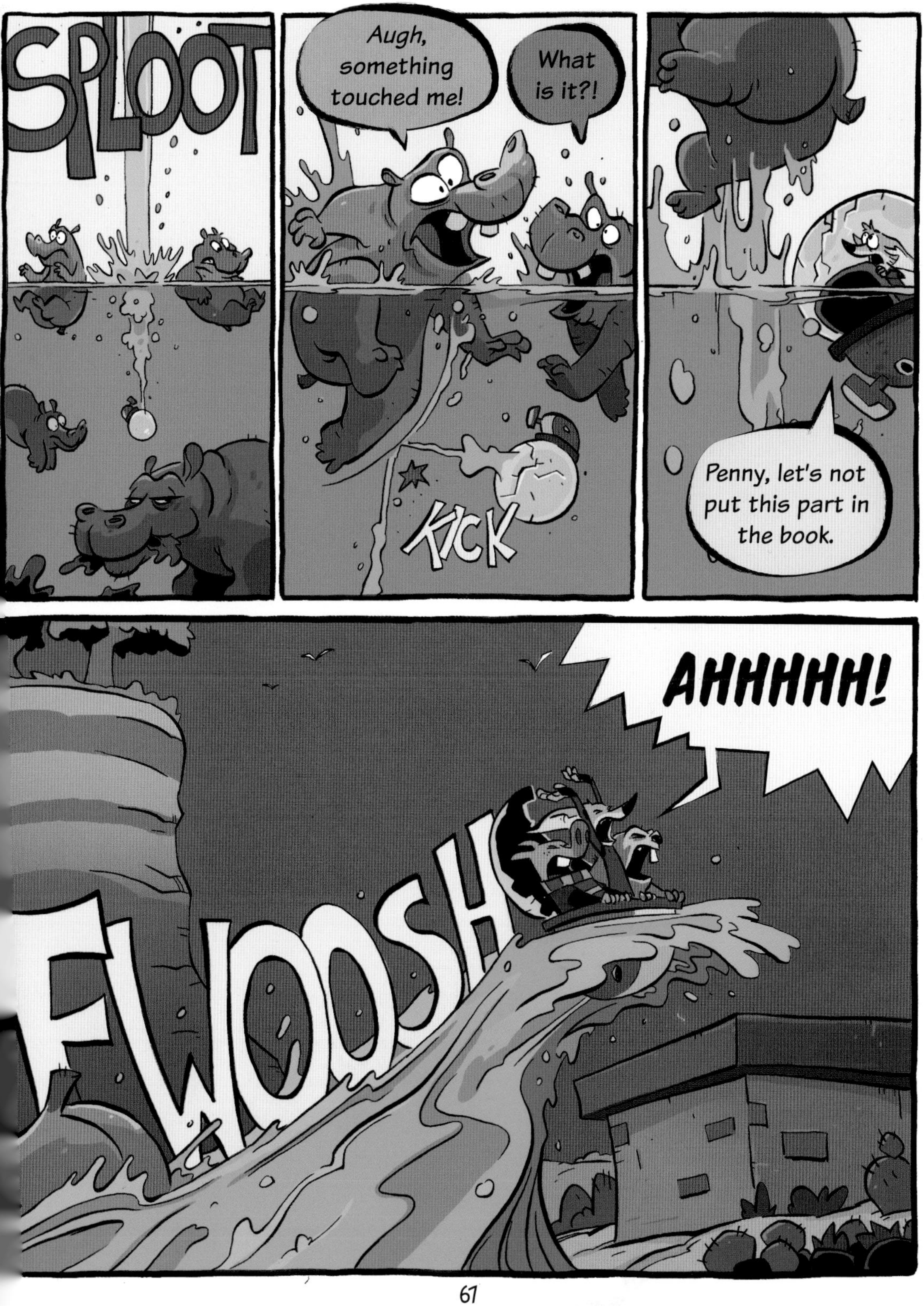
SPLOOT
Augh, something touched me!
What is it?!
KICK
Penny, let's not put this part in the book.
AHHHHH!
WOOSH

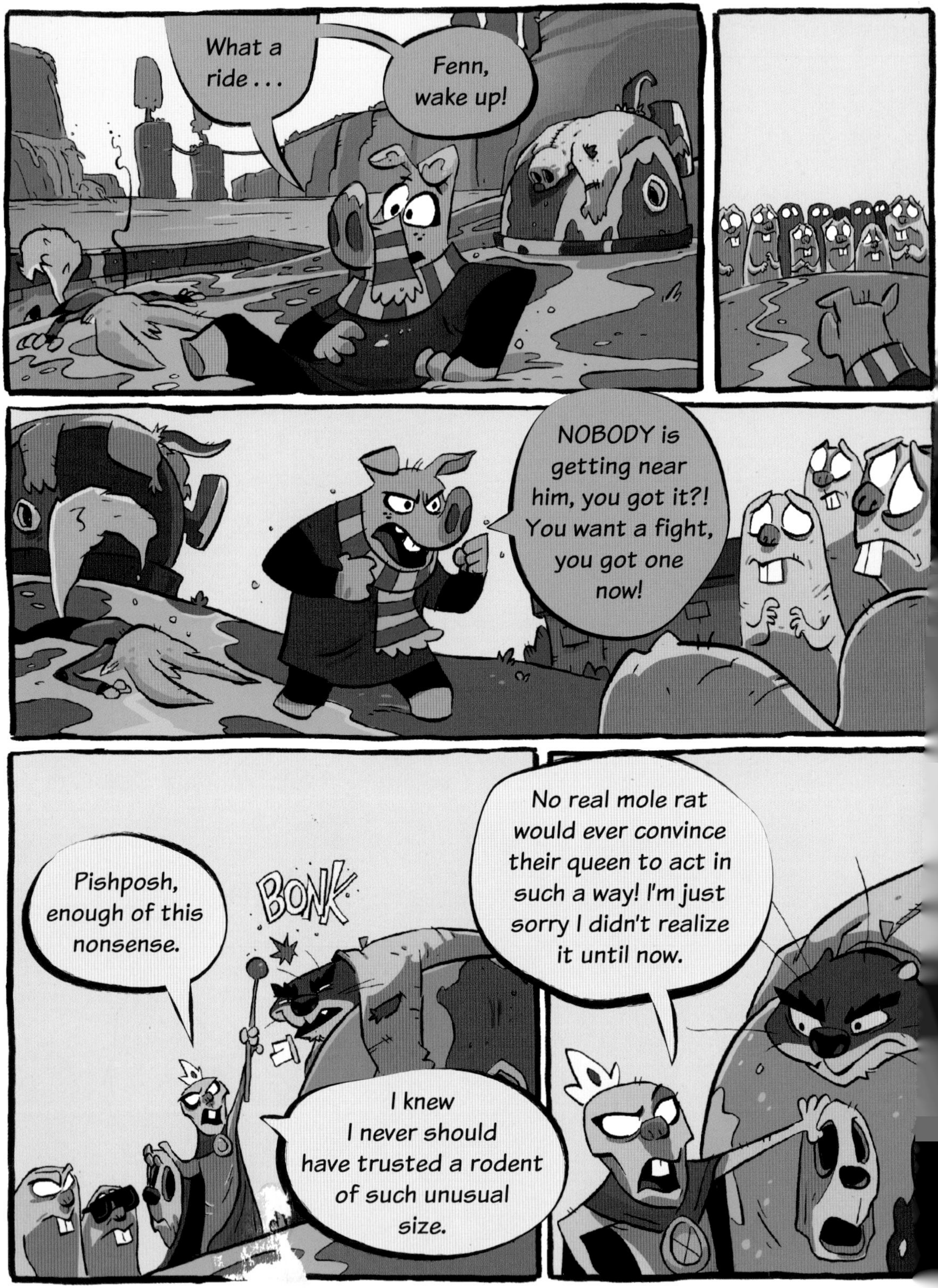
What a ride . . .
Fenn, wake up!
NOBODY is getting near him, you got it?! You want a fight, you got one now!
Pishposh, enough of this nonsense.
BONK
I knew I never should have trusted a rodent of such unusual size.
No real mole rat would ever convince their queen to act in such a way! I'm just sorry I didn't realize it until now.

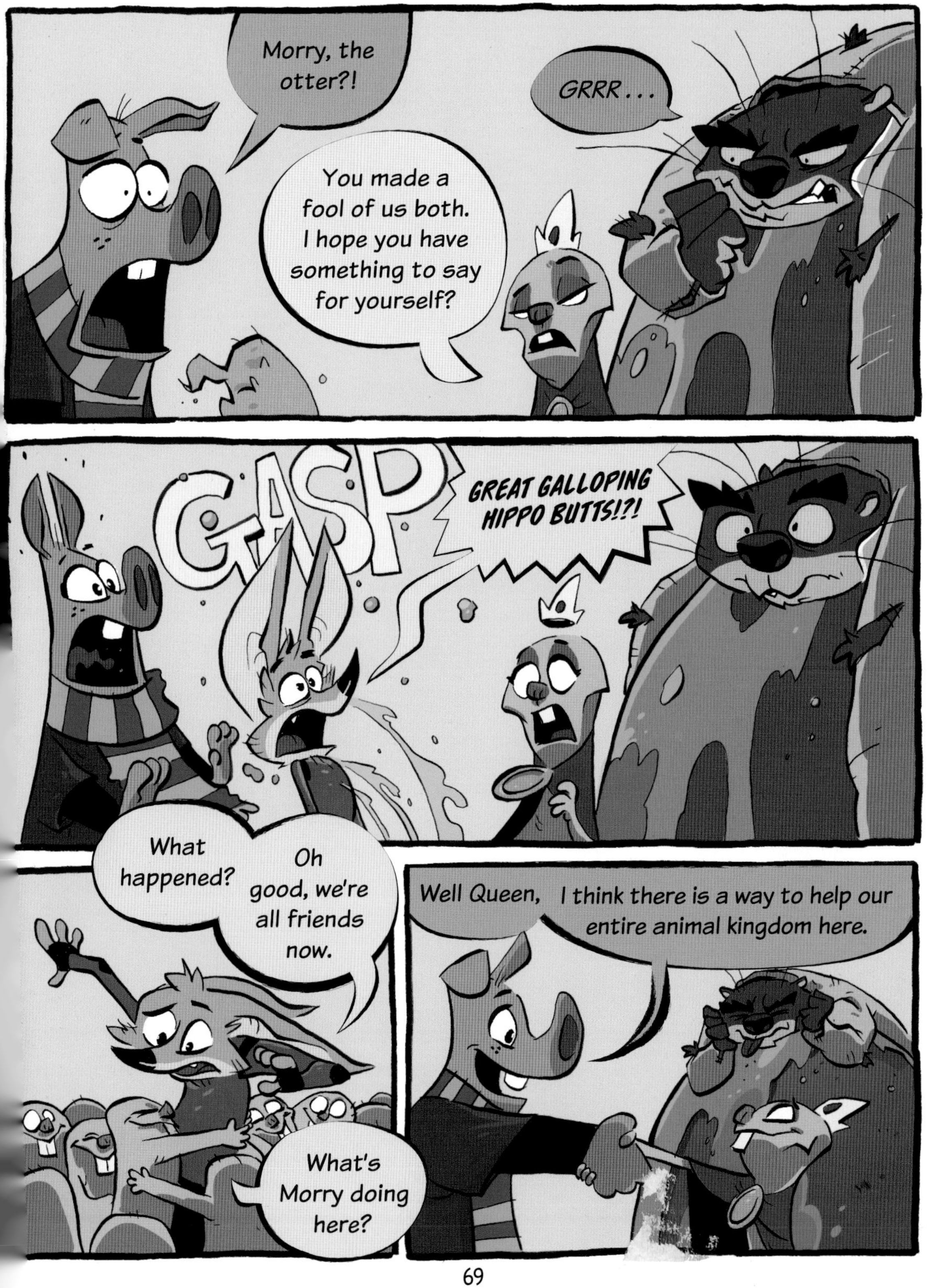
Morry, the otter?!
GRRR...
You made a fool of us both. I hope you have something to say for yourself?
GASP
GREAT GALLOPING HIPPO BUTTS!?!
What happened?
Oh good, we're all friends now.
What's Morry doing here?
Well Queen,
I think there is a way to help our entire animal kingdom here.

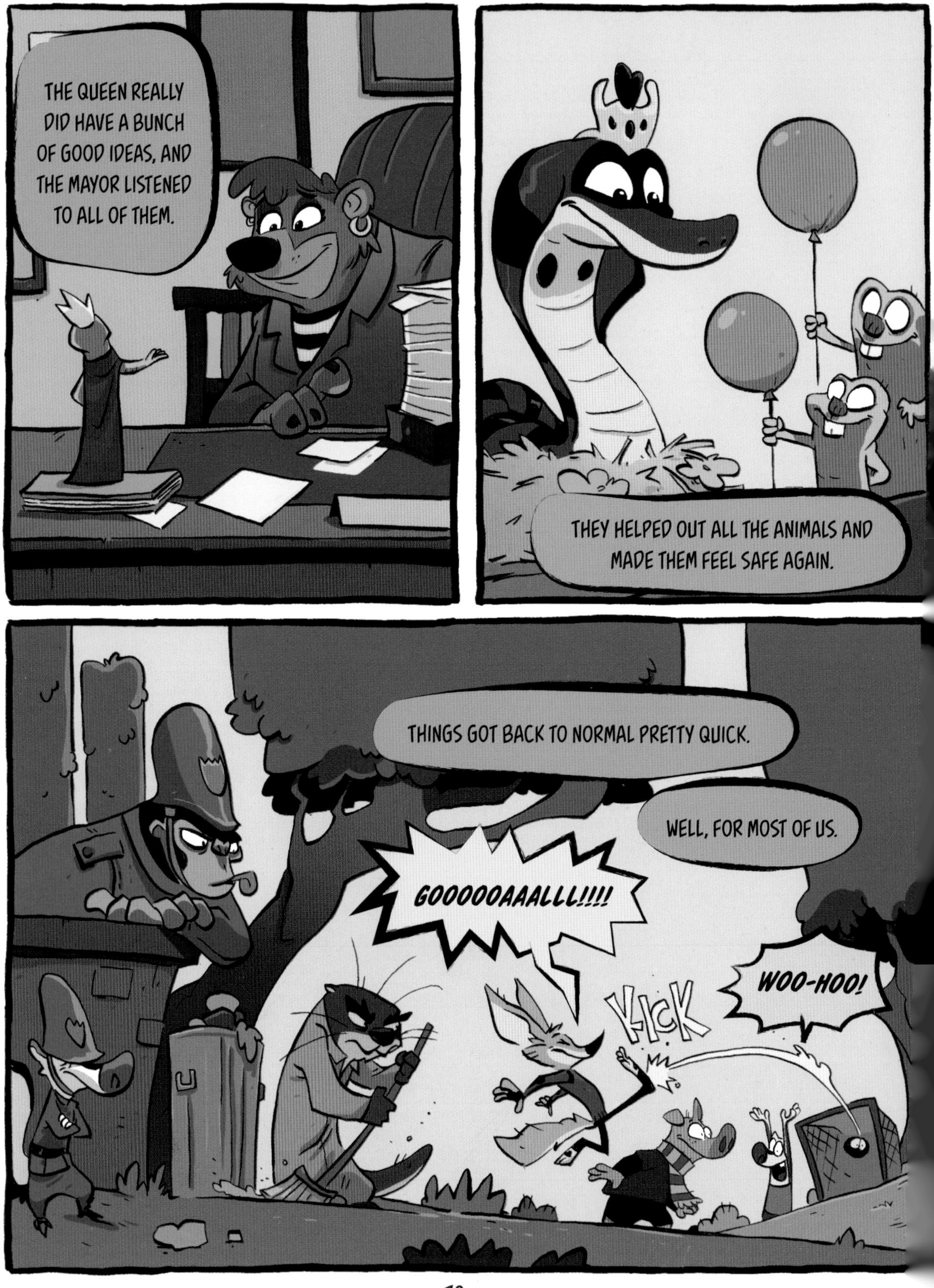
THE QUEEN REALLY DID HAVE A BUNCH OF GOOD IDEAS, AND THE MAYOR LISTENED TO ALL OF THEM.
THEY HELPED OUT ALL THE ANIMALS AND MADE THEM FEEL SAFE AGAIN.
THINGS GOT BACK TO NORMAL PRETTY QUICK.
WELL, FOR MOST OF US.
GOOOOOAAALLL!!!!
KICK
WOO-HOO!

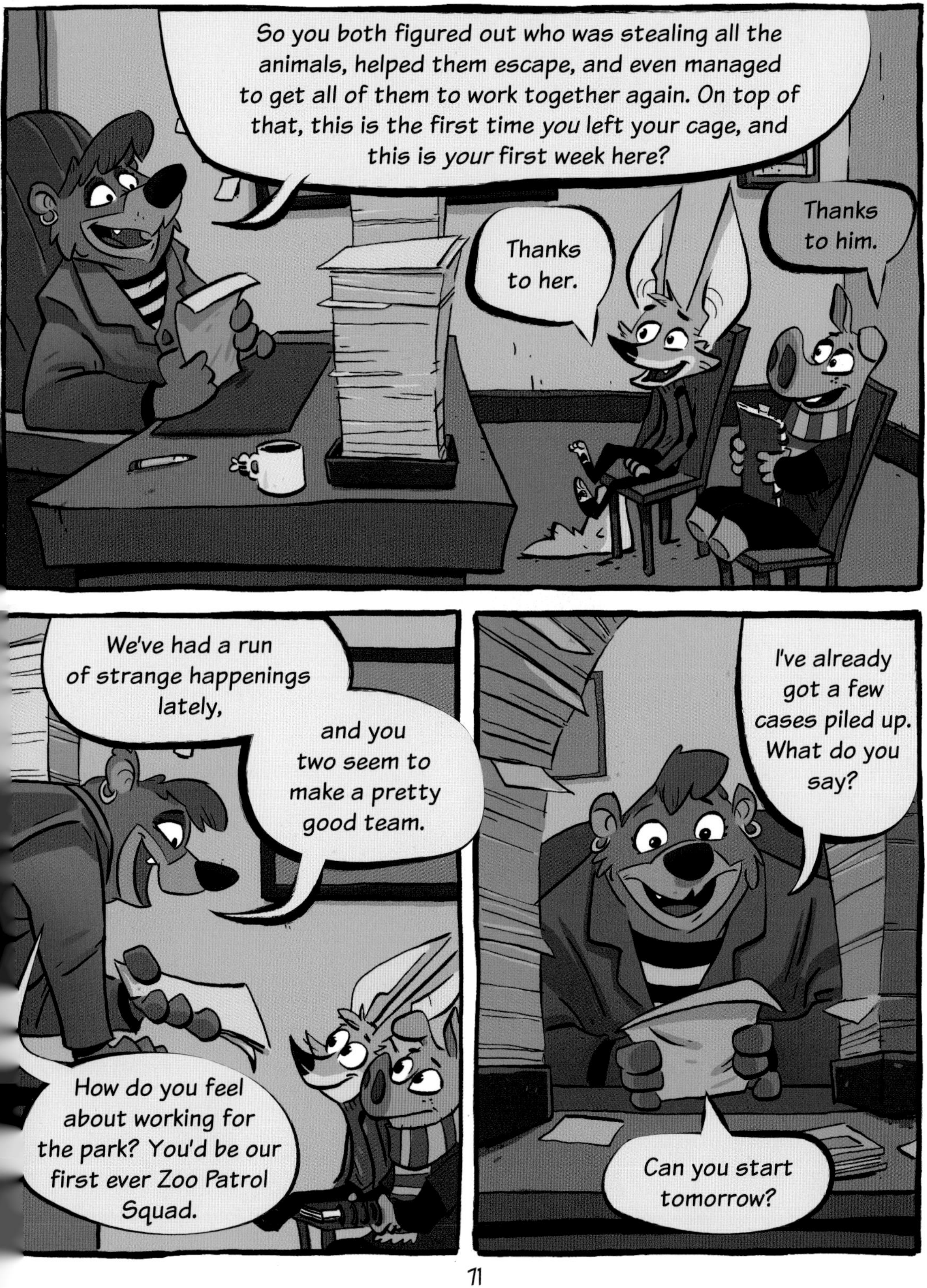

So you both figured out who was stealing all the animals, helped them escape, and even managed to get all of them to work together again. On top of that, this is the first time *you* left your cage, and this is *your* first week here?
Thanks to her.
Thanks to him.
We've had a run of strange happenings lately,
and you two seem to make a pretty good team.
How do you feel about working for the park? You'd be our first ever Zoo Patrol Squad.
I've already got a few cases piled up. What do you say?
Can you start tomorrow?

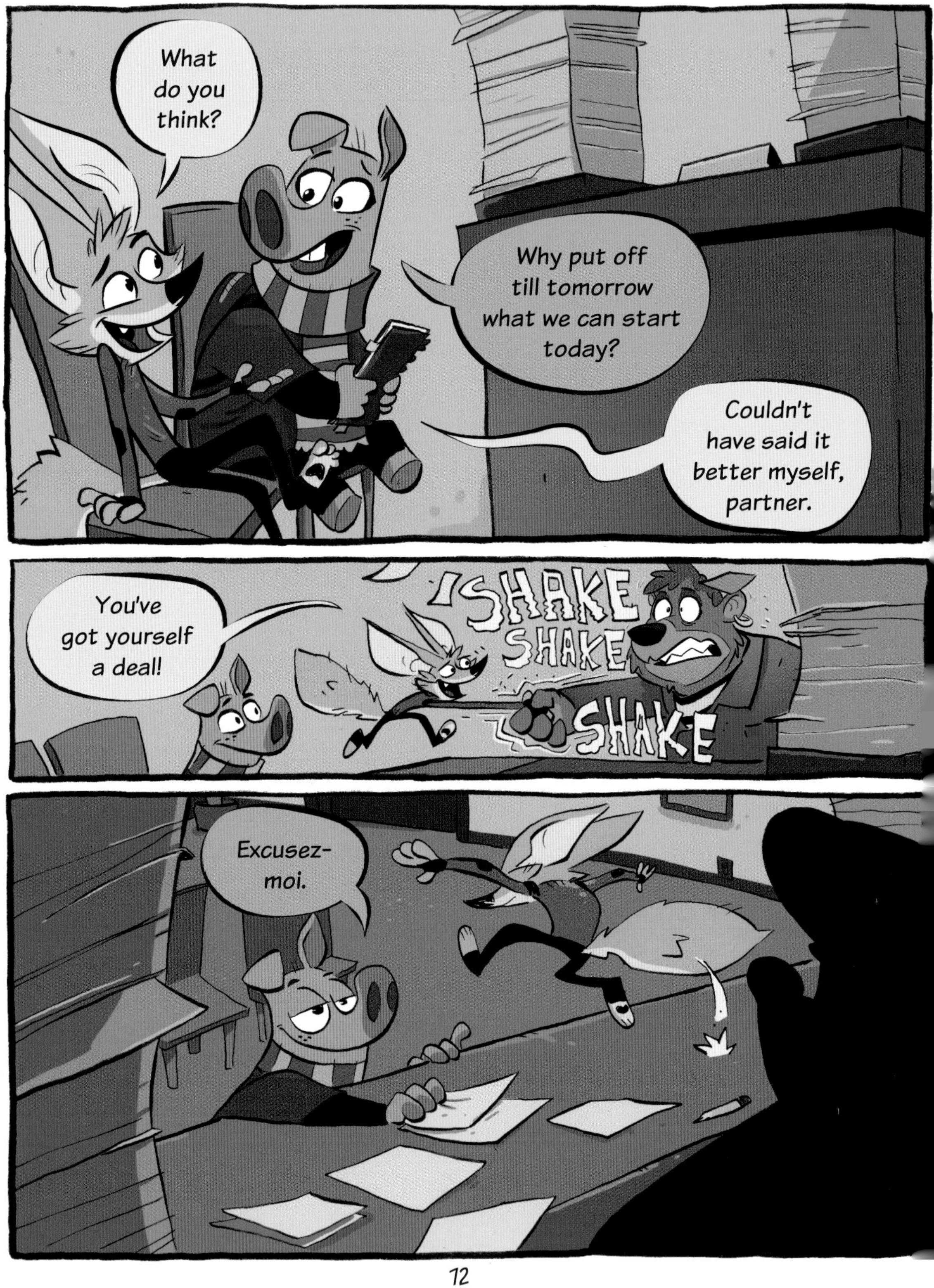

What do you think?
Why put off till tomorrow what we can start today?
Couldn't have said it better myself, partner.
You've got yourself a deal!
SHAKE
SHAKE
SHAKE
Excusez-moi.

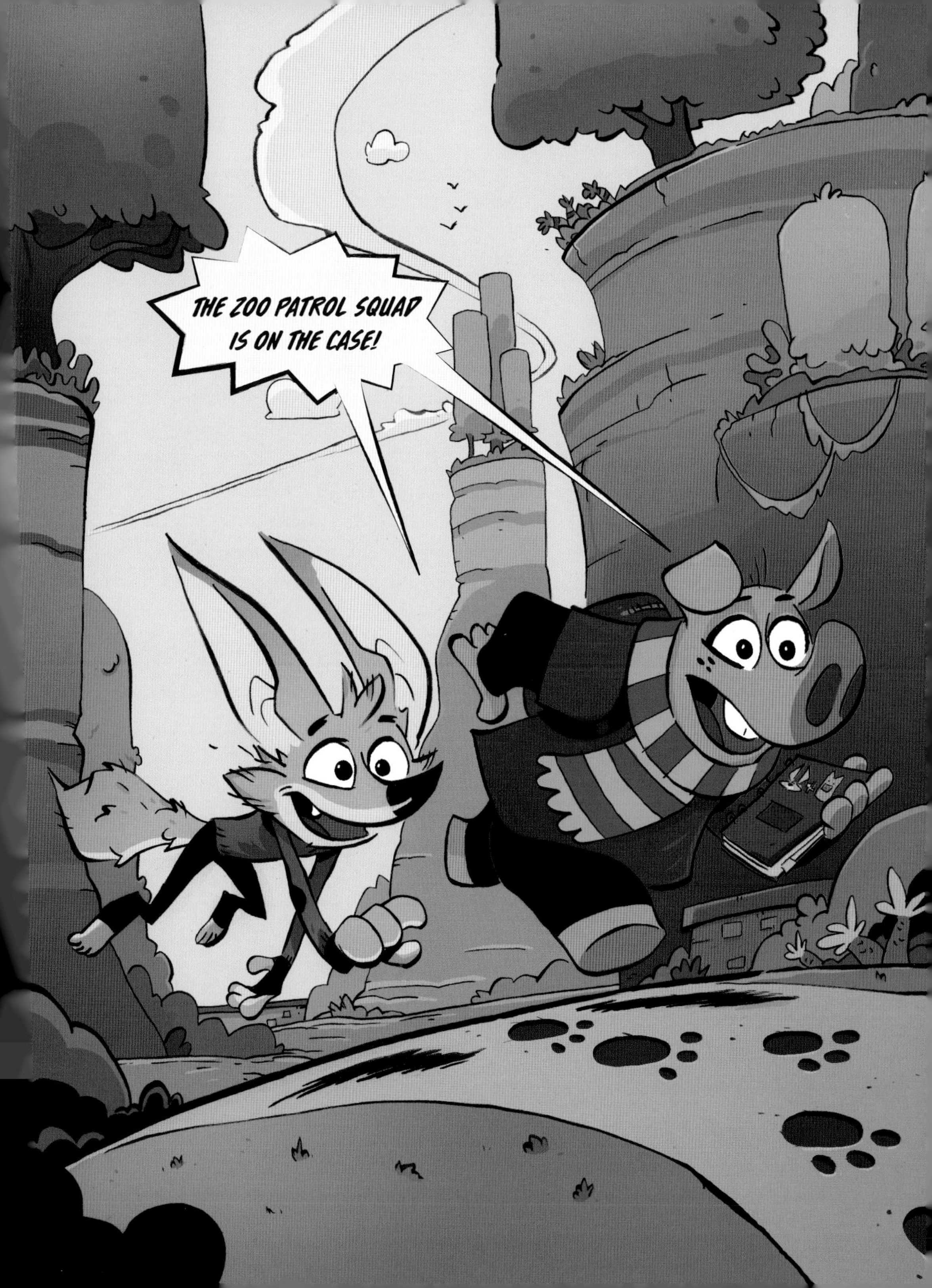
THE ZOO PATROL SQUAD
IS ON THE CASE!

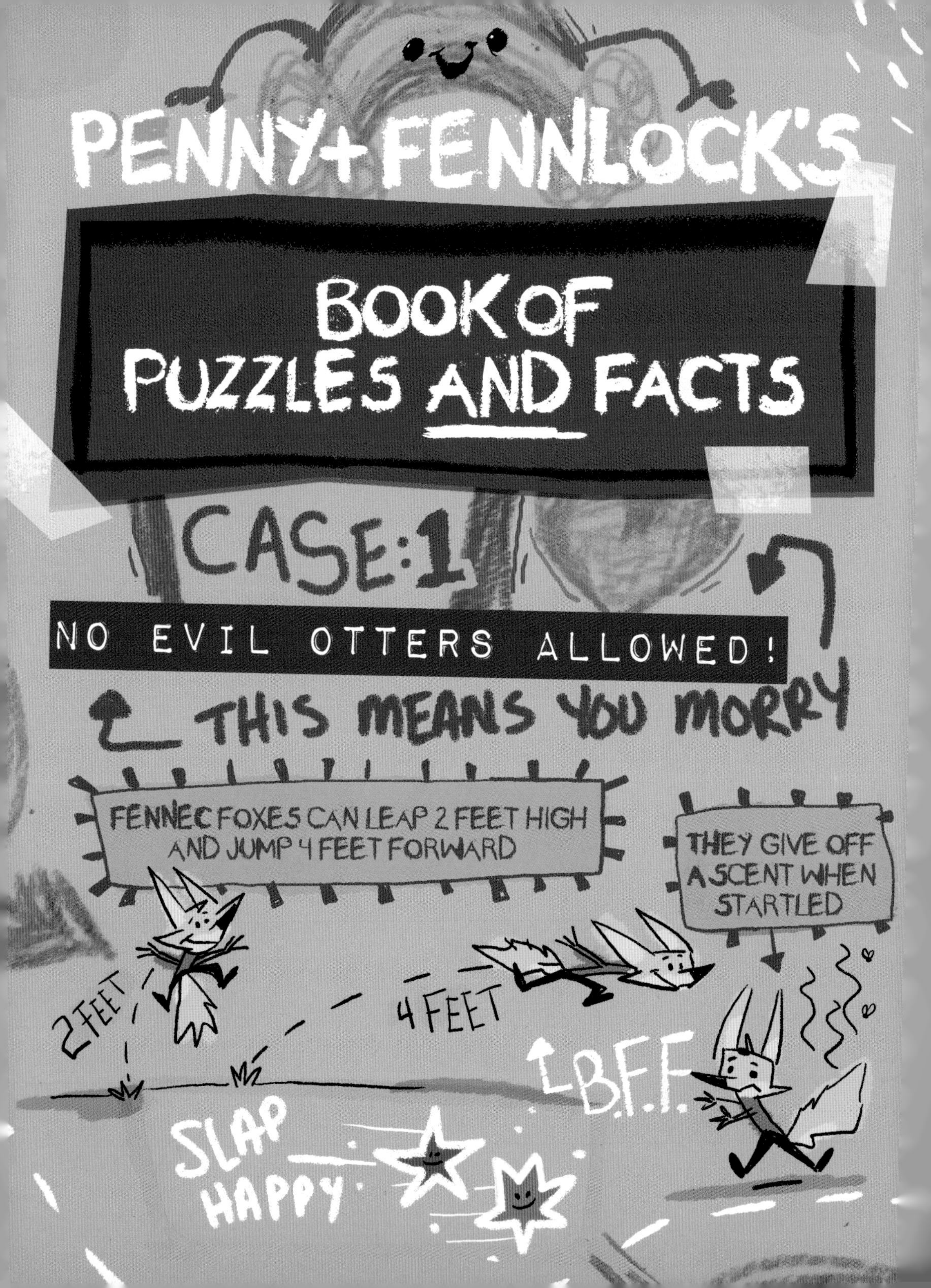
PENNY + FENNLOCK'S
BOOK OF PUZZLES AND FACTS
CASE: 1
NO EVIL OTTERS ALLOWED!
THIS MEANS YOU MORRY
FENNEC FOXES CAN LEAP 2 FEET HIGH AND JUMP 4 FEET FORWARD
THEY GIVE OFF A SCENT WHEN STARTLED
2 FEET
4 FEET
B.F.F.
SLAP HAPPY

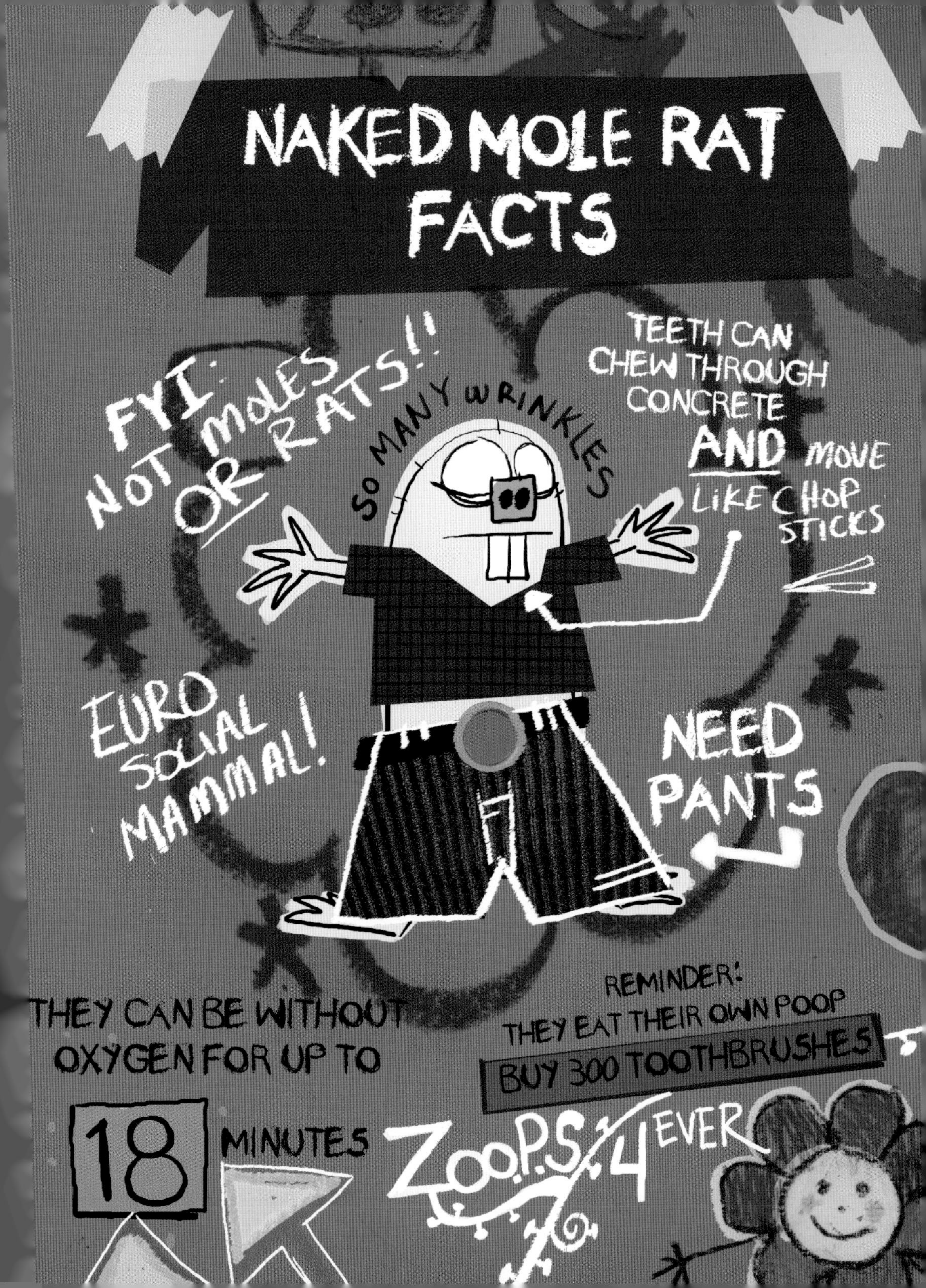
NAKED MOLE RAT FACTS
FYI: NOT MOLES OR RATS!!
SO MANY WRINKLES
TEETH CAN CHEW THROUGH CONCRETE AND MOVE LIKE CHOP STICKS
EURO SOCIAL MAMMAL!
NEED PANTS
THEY CAN BE WITHOUT OXYGEN FOR UP TO
18 MINUTES
REMINDER: THEY EAT THEIR OWN POOP
BUY 300 TOOTHBRUSHES
ZOO.P.S. 4 EVER

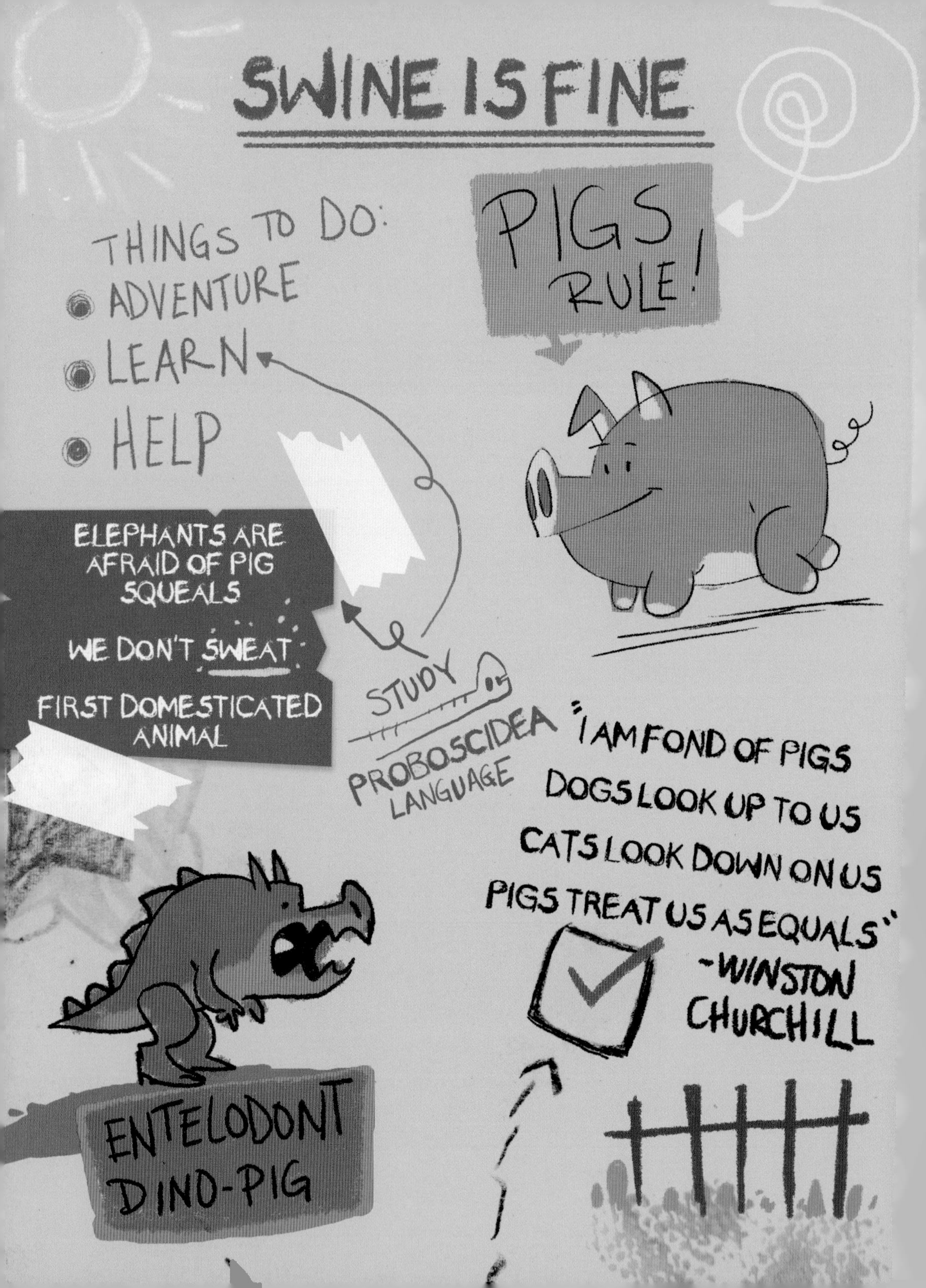
SWINE IS FINE
THINGS TO DO:
ADVENTURE
LEARN
HELP
PIGS RULE!
ELEPHANTS ARE AFRAID OF PIG SQUEALS
WE DON'T SWEAT
FIRST DOMESTICATED ANIMAL
STUDY
PROBOSCIDEA LANGUAGE
"I AM FOND OF PIGS
DOGS LOOK UP TO US
CATS LOOK DOWN ON US
PIGS TREAT US AS EQUALS"
~WINSTON CHURCHILL
ENTELODONT DINO-PIG

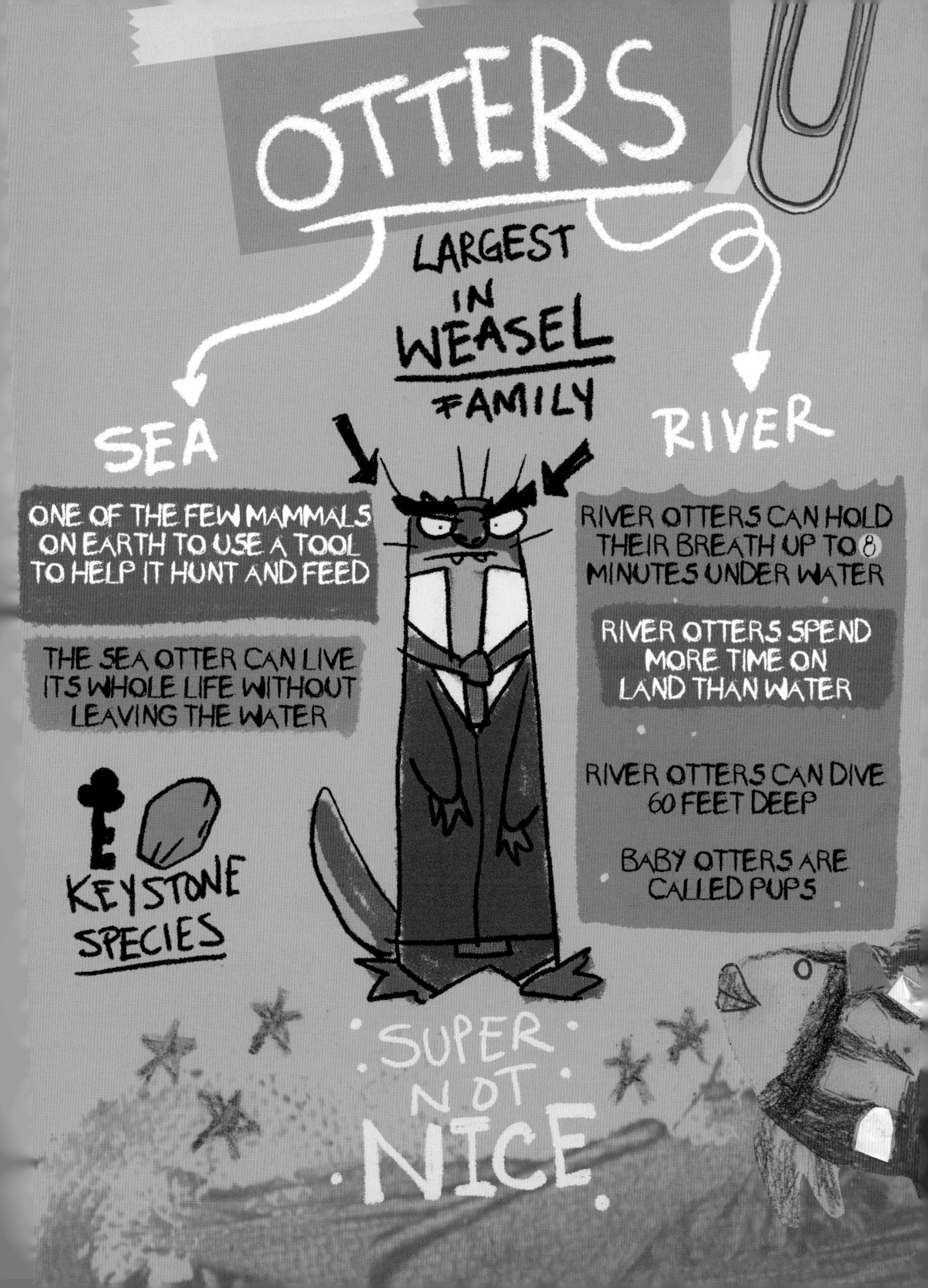
OTTERS
LARGEST IN WEASEL FAMILY
SEA
RIVER
ONE OF THE FEW MAMMALS ON EARTH TO USE A TOOL TO HELP IT HUNT AND FEED
THE SEA OTTER CAN LIVE ITS WHOLE LIFE WITHOUT LEAVING THE WATER
KEYSTONE SPECIES
RIVER OTTERS CAN HOLD THEIR BREATH UP TO 8 MINUTES UNDER WATER
RIVER OTTERS SPEND MORE TIME ON LAND THAN WATER
RIVER OTTERS CAN DIVE 60 FEET DEEP
BABY OTTERS ARE CALLED PUPS
SUPER NOT NICE

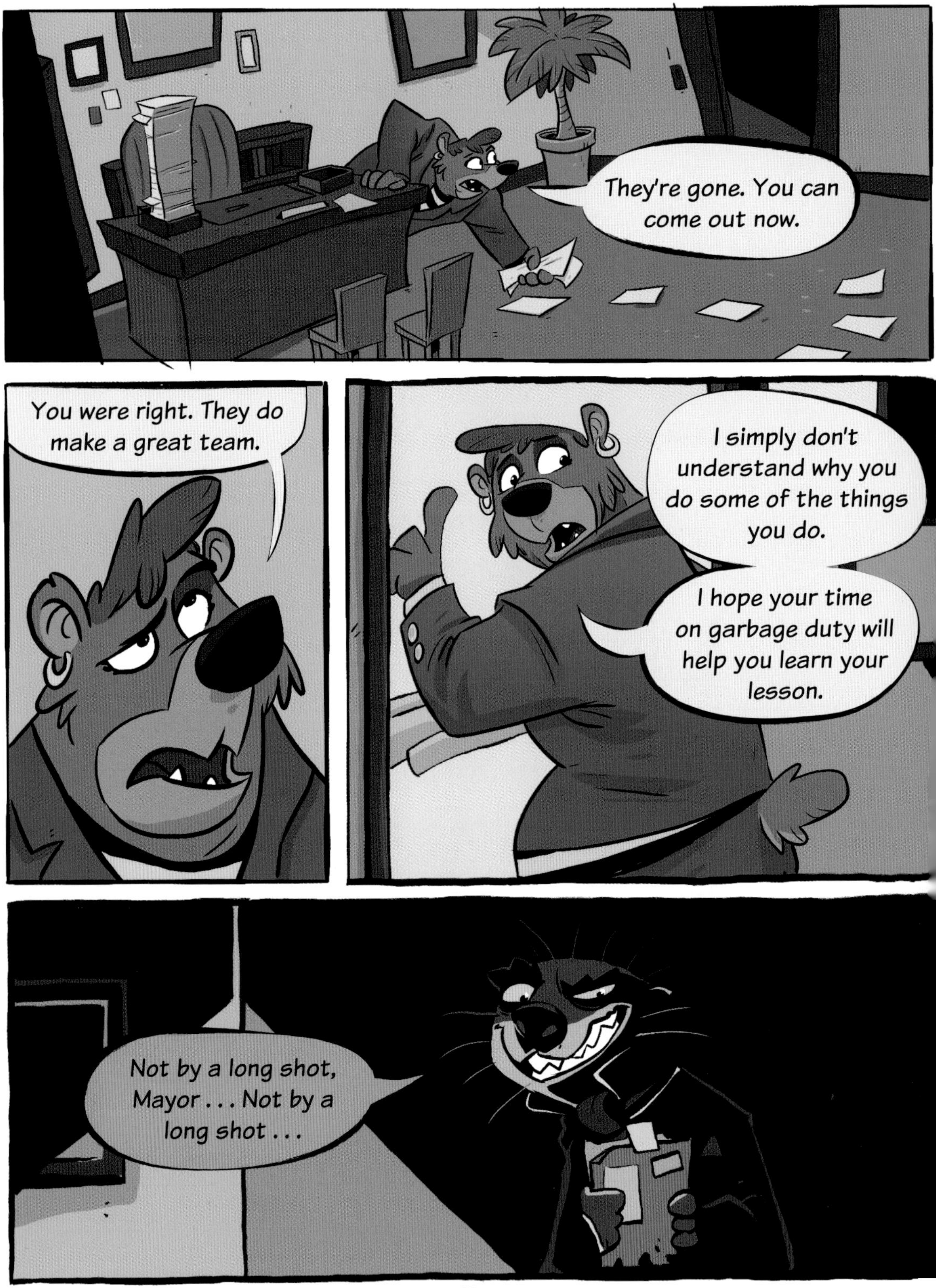
They're gone. You can come out now.
You were right. They do make a great team.
I simply don't understand why you do some of the things you do.
I hope your time on garbage duty will help you learn your lesson.
Not by a long shot, Mayor . . . Not by a long shot . . .